THE GALLOWS IN MY GARDEN

Grace Lawson and her brother Donald stand to inherit their late father's millions when they reach the age of twenty-one — but someone in their household of family, servants and regular guests seems intent on ensuring they don't live that long. Donald disappears, and a would-be killer dogs Grace's every move. Not wanting to involve the police and create a family scandal, Grace turns to private investigator Manville Moon — who is unaware of how complex the case will be, or that his own life will be threatened . . .

RICHARD DEMING

THE GALLOWS IN MY GARDEN

Complete and Unabridged

LINFORD
Leicester

First published in Great Britain

First Linford Edition
published 2016

A catalogue record for this book is available
from the British Library.

ISBN 978–1–4448–2842–9

Published by
F. A. Thorpe (Publishing)
Anstey, Leicestershire

Set by Words & Graphics Ltd.
Anstey, Leicestershire
Printed and bound in Great Britain by
T. J. International Ltd., Padstow, Cornwall

This book is printed on acid-free paper

TO MY MOTHER
who would prefer me to write
innocuous tales about members of
Dover Place Church

'The gallows in my garden, people say,
Is new and neat and adequately tall.
I tie the noose on in a knowing way
As one that knots his necktie for a ball;
But just as all the neighbors . . . on the
    wall . . .
Are drawing a long breath to shout
    'Hurray!'
The strangest whim has seized me . . .
    After all
I think I will not hang myself today.'

From G. K. Chesterton's
A Ballade of Suicide

1

It was a Saturday in the middle of July, and the brick courtyard next to my bedroom gathered all the heat it could absorb from a bright sun and shoved it through my window.

I was therefore sleeping naked without covers when the most beautiful woman I ever met dropped in at high noon.

It takes me longer to get from bed to the door than most people, because I first have to strap on an intricate contrivance of cork, aluminum, and leather which substitutes for the lower part of a right leg I contributed to the war effort. As a result, I was still nude when a soprano voice from the front room called, 'Anybody home?'

'Stay where you are!' I yelled, then added in a lower tone, 'Unless you've had children and are over seventy.'

A girlish giggle indicated my caller was somewhat less than seventy, so I advised her to wait ten minutes while I made myself presentable. It was closer to fifteen before I accomplished this chore, including a rapid shave. I always shave before investigating female callers who get me out of bed, because a bent nose and one drooping eyelid is enough handicap for a face, without adding whiskers.

When I finally emerged from the bedroom, I found her standing before the mantel in my front room. It is hard to describe the first impact of her beauty, and useless to try to catalogue its details, for no one of her attributes would have been outstanding in a crowd of any hundred college-age girls. She was about nineteen or twenty, of average height, average slimness, average blondeness of hair and blueness of eye.

Yet some wondrous alchemy combined her various average features into an effect which was shattering. Perhaps it was partly her appearance of crisp coolness in an oppressive heat that had already begun to wilt my fresh collar. Whatever it was, it caught me between the horns like a club, although from the advanced senility of my thirty-two years I rarely glance twice at women under voting age.

'My name is Grace Lawson,' she said. 'You're Mr. Moon?'

'I think so,' I said, still off-center. 'Please take a seat.' I led her to my favorite chair and released her hand only after she sat down. 'Have a drink?' I asked, fumbling with the rye decanter, then changing my mind. 'No, you're too young. Smoke?'

'No, thanks,' she said, smiling. Apparently she was used to men stumbling over their own feet when they first met her.

I said, 'Pardon me,' poured breakfast into a shot glass, tossed it off, lit a cigar, and regained my equilibrium. When I took a seat on the sofa across from her, I found I could regard her without shooting any embolisms.

'You've come on business,' I said. 'That's a deduction. Pretty girls never call on me socially.'

'You're probably being modest.' She smiled. 'But I did come on business. Do you charge much?'

'More than I'm worth. Tell me what you want before we discuss rates.'

3

'I couldn't pay very much,' she said. 'I don't get my money until I'm twenty-one, and all I have is five hundred a month allowance.'

I blinked. 'You're virtually a pauper. How old did you say you are?'

'Going on twenty.'

'In school somewhere?'

'The state university summer session. I had to make up two courses I dropped. I'm a junior.'

'Where'd you hear of me?'

'The woman who owns El Patio recommended you. The night club, you know.'

'Fausta Moreni?' I asked.

'Yes, Fausta. Arnold and I have dinner at El Patio now and then. We were telling Fausta about the attempts on my life, and she recommended I see you.' She smiled faintly. 'She said if I made eyes at you, she'd cut my heart out, but she was only fooling.'

'You don't know Fausta,' I told her. 'Let's start at the beginning. Somebody's trying to kill you?'

'I think so. Once the saddle girth on my

riding-horse was cut, presumably so I'd fall; and once my milk was poisoned; and once a flowerpot fell from an upper window when I was coming in late at night, and it broke right next to me.'

I sat up straight. 'You're lucky you're alive! How'd you escape all that?'

'Just luck, really,' she said. 'The saddle girth was cut so far it snapped soon as my weight hit the stirrup. And the milk was poisoned with something that smelled strong, so I didn't even taste it. Uncle Doug had it analyzed — he's a doctor, you know — but I've forgotten what the poison was. Of course, maybe the flowerpot was just an accident. It missed me by several feet.'

'You report all this to the police?'

'Oh, no. You see, it almost has to be someone in the house, so we wouldn't want the papers to get it. Uncle Doug has been sort of investigating, but since Don ran away last week, Arnold and I have been wondering if that's enough. We think maybe someone tried to kill Don, too, and he ran away because he was scared.'

'Who's Don?' I asked, somewhat

numbed by the barrage of names she had just thrown at me.

'My brother.'

'Wait a minute,' I said. 'Your name is Grace Lawson? The kid who disappeared last week is your brother?'

'My older brother, though not much older. Don was born just eleven months before I was. Last Sunday he left a note and ran off without even taking a suitcase.'

I asked, 'Aren't you and your brother scheduled to inherit Fort Knox or something at twenty-one? I didn't read the news item on it very carefully.'

'We each get some money at twenty-one,' she admitted. 'Unless whoever is after us succeeds in killing us. Then it goes to Ann.'

I held up one palm. 'For some reason you only confuse me, the more you talk. Begin by telling me all about yourself and your family.'

'Well, there's not very much about me,' she said. 'I go to State U, but I live at home and drive back and forth. It's only fifteen miles, you know. We live in Willow

6

Dale. My mother died when I was born, and Daddy was killed in an auto accident a year ago. Ann is my stepmother, but I call her Ann because she's only twelve years older than me, and more like a pal than a mother. Uncle Doug is Dr. Douglas Lawson, Daddy's younger brother. He's a bachelor and a regular dream, and if he weren't my uncle and I weren't in love with Arnold, I'd marry him even though he is an elderly man of forty.'

Momentarily I contemplated the eight years remaining between me and the wheelchair, then asked, 'Uncle Doug live in the house?'

'No. Well, in a way. He has an apartment in town, but he visits so much we gave him his own room. He's always there weekends. But just Ann, Don, and I really live there.'

I said slowly, 'A minute ago you said whoever is trying to kill you must live in the house. You mean Ann?'

'Oh, no!' she said quickly. 'It couldn't possibly be Ann. Though she, Don, and I are the only real residents, we have lots of regular visitors. There's Mr. Mannering, the family lawyer. He has his own room, too. And Arnold. And Abigail Stoltz, the painter. She's an aunt of Ann's and visits weekends a lot. And Gerald Cushing, who runs the drugstore chain for the estate. Daddy started the Lawson Drug chain, you know. Then there are five servants. All those people were around when the attempts were made on me.'

'Who is this Arnold you're in love with?'

'My fiancé. Arnold Tate. He's a graduate student in English Lit at State U. He's going to be a professor, and eventually a university president.'

'Going to buy him a university?'

'Oh, no,' she said, wide-eyed. 'Arnold wouldn't permit that. We even have to live on his salary after we get married, though I can use my money to educate the children if I want.'

'OK, now tell me about the will. How is the money set up?'

She frowned slightly. 'I don't believe the will has anything to do with someone trying to kill me.'

'Maybe not,' I said, 'but tell me anyway.'

'Well,' she said reluctantly, 'it seems Daddy wanted to be sure we children got the big share, though I don't think it was very nice of him not to trust Ann to do the right thing. She's awfully nice, really. Of course he provided for her. She has income for life from a half-million-dollar trust fund, and the use of the house as long as she wants, though she can't sell it. Even the house's maintenance is provided for through another trust fund, so Ann doesn't have to worry about taxes or upkeep or servants' salaries or anything. Then there were some bequests to charities, and fifty thousand dollars to Uncle Doug, and ten thousand dollars, I think it was, to Maggie, the housekeeper. The rest is held in trust for Don and me, or the survivor if one dies, until we reach twenty-one, when we each get half, providing we don't marry before that.'

'How was that last again?' I asked.

'That was because Don ran off and married a waitress when he was eighteen,' she said. 'He was always a little wild. Daddy had it annulled, and according to the will, if either of us marries before twenty-one, we get only one hundred thousand dollars and the rest goes to the other. If we both marry, or both die, Ann gets the bulk of the estate and all the trust funds are sort of canceled out.'

'I see. How much is the bulk of the estate?'

'I don't remember exactly. Once I asked Mr. Mannering, but I forget whether he said eight or eighteen million.'

I got up and poured myself another drink. 'Just offhand,' I said, 'it looks like Don has the best motive for knocking you off, and your stepmother has the best motive for quenching you both.'

'Oh, no,' she objected. 'Ann doesn't even know about the attempts on my life.' I noticed her objection did not extend to brother Don, which rather intrigued me.

'Who does know?' I asked.

'Only Arnold and Uncle Doug. I don't think it has anything to do with the will. I think probably one of the servants is insane.'

'That's a sound theory,' I agreed. 'Let's hire a psychiatrist to psychoanalyze everybody. What is it you want me to do now? Act as a bodyguard?'

'Well, I thought you could sort of investigate around to find out what's going on. You're a private detective, aren't you?'

Generally I say yes when a potential client asks me that, but to my own amazement I found myself telling the truth. 'Theoretically. But I specialize in bodyguarding. You might call me a professional bodyguard.'

'The card under your doorbell reads, 'Manville Moon, Confidential Investigations.''

'All right,' I said. 'Confidential Investigations' sounds better than 'Professional Bodyguard.' I'd be glad to guard your body for a fee, but investigation of the attempts on your life ought to be made by the police.'

Her lower lip thrust out. 'Fausta Moreni said you made investigations like this. She said you even solved some murders.'

'I have on occasion,' I said patiently. 'But always when the police were on the case, too. If I start poking around for a potential murderer without the cops knowing anything about it, and he happens to get you before I get him, the district attorney is going to ask nasty questions. The state doesn't issue private detective licenses because it thinks the regular police need competition. Private dicks are supposed to supplement police work, not substitute for it.'

She looked disappointed. 'I thought maybe you could come up as a guest, say a friend of Arnold's, and sort of look around without exciting anybody.'

'You can't get to the bottom of a thing like this without asking questions. I'd have to check the people who handled the poisoned milk, whoever saddled your horse, who was awake when the flowerpot dropped. You think a casual house guest who starts prying like that isn't going to excite anyone?'

'Well, gee,' she said uncertainly. 'I wouldn't want to call the police without checking with Uncle Doug first.' She frowned, then she threw one of her stupefying smiles directly into my face. 'Would you come up just over the weekend and look around?

12

Then Monday we'll either let the police know, or I'll release you.'

Before I could recover from the smile, I heard myself saying, 'I suppose I could do that.'

She rose in preparation to leave. 'I'll drive back to school and pick up Arnold. I'm supposed to be in class now, but I cut. We'll come by for you about six. Supposedly you'll be driving down from the university with us, in case anyone at home asks. I guess you'd better be a graduate student in English literature, too, so Arnold can cover for you if anyone asks you questions about Shakespeare or something.'

'All right,' I said. 'I read Shakespeare in high school. Imagine I'll be able to fool the servants, anyway.'

After she left I remembered I had never told her my rates, which indicates the effect she had on people.

2

Fausta Moreni is the only woman I ever got excited enough about to want to marry, but that was a long time ago. We met when I was twenty-four and she was a nineteen-year-old refugee from fascist Italy. From Rome on north, Italians are neither as dark-skinned nor black-haired as the southern variety, which constitutes most of America's Italo-American population. Fausta was from Rome and she had snapping brown eyes, light tan skin, and vivid blonde hair.

All during the war I carried her picture in my wallet and the memory of her comic accent, quick movements, and soft lips somewhere inside me. The trouble was, my memory was of a naïve youngster bewildered by a strange country and needing a strong man's protection. But when I finally returned home Fausta wasn't in need of anything. She had become, peculiarly enough, a professional blackjack dealer, and one of the highest paid in the country at that. Possibly her success was due as much to her opponents' concentrating only half their minds on the cards and the other half on trying to beat down her resistance to their personal designs as it was to pure skill, but nevertheless her employer thought enough of her to leave her El Patio when he suddenly departed with a bullet through his head.

No sooner had the will been read than Fausta closed the casino and converted El Patio into a restaurant/night club. It was a smart move, for not only was the legitimate business less precarious, but it made as much in the long run by charging outrageous prices, and Fausta was an extremely rich woman at twenty-seven.

I think I must like my women weak and helpless, for the change was more than I could take. More or less by mutual consent we stopped mentioning marriage, but though we rarely saw each other these days, we were still good friends, and I have never been able to generate for any other woman the same feeling I once had for Fausta.

After Grace Lawson departed, I took a cold shower, had lunch at the corner drugstore, then returned to my apartment and phoned Fausta at El Patio.

'Manny!' her husky voice said. 'Why do you never phone unless I send you a customer? You do not like Fausta's kisses anymore?'

'I love 'em like candy,' I said. 'What's the dope on this Lawson girl?'

'She is a nice girl and her boy Arnold is very nice, too. You take good care of her, you hear? And keep it strictly business. She is much too young for an old man like you.'

'Don't you ever think of anything but the passes I make at other women?' I asked.

'Of course not,' Fausta said. 'You stop making passes and I will stop thinking about it.'

'All right. What you know about the kid?'

'Only that she and her Arnold have dinner here now and then. Also someone

16

is trying to kill her, but I do not know who.'

'You're not much help,' I said, 'but thanks for the business. See you later, Fausta.'

'Wait, Manny! When will you come to see me?'

'One of these nights.'

'You said that a month ago,' she complained. 'You come tonight.'

'Sorry. Going to the Lawsons' for the weekend.'

'Then you come Monday.'

'Maybe,' I said. 'I'll give you a ring.'

By the time I finished packing my smallest grip, it was only two o'clock and I had nothing to do until Grace Lawson returned at six. For the next three hours I skimmed over my copy of *Hamlet* in preparation for my role as an English student, on the theory that most people remembered little aside from *Hamlet* of the classics they were exposed to in school. Then the doorbell rang.

My caller was a tall, heavy-boned man who looked like an English lord. He stood so straight he nearly leaned backward,

17

and held his head back even farther, so that condescending eyes peered down his nose as though through invisible bifocals. He was dressed in white gabardine, white shoes, and a sailor straw hat, and hands thrust deeply into his coat pockets pulled the cloth tightly across an ominous bulge under his arm.

When he spoke, the English-lord effect was destroyed by a pure midwestern accent.

'You Manville Moon?' he asked.

I admitted I was and stepped aside to let him enter.

'You can call me Tom Jones because that's not my name,' he said, and drew wide lips back in a humorless grin to expose horse-sized teeth.

Without offering his hand, he placed his straw hat on the mantel and appropriated the most comfortable chair in the room.

I said, 'Excuse me a minute,' went into the bedroom, removed the P-38 and shoulder holster I had packed in my grip, and arranged them where they would be more readily accessible.

18

When I rejoined the man who was not Tom Jones, he asked without preamble, 'Could you use five thousand dollars, Moon?'

'Who couldn't?' I said.

'Good. A plane leaves for Mexico City in an hour. You get a month's vacation with all expenses paid, plus five thousand bucks. Better start packing.'

'What do I do to earn it?'

'Nothing.' He exposed his horsy teeth again. 'It's a new radio giveaway program. Only instead of asking you questions, we just ask you not to ask us questions.'

'No thanks,' I said. 'I couldn't afford the income tax on five thousand dollars.'

'Did I say five?' he asked. 'I meant ten.'

'You could mean a million and I wouldn't bite.'

'Then let me put it another way,' he said agreeably. 'You get ten thousand and a free vacation, or nothing and a free funeral. Catch on, Moon?'

'Sure. You're new in town, aren't you?'

He gave me his humorless grin. 'About a week.'

'Then you don't know about my

double standard. You see, I divide everybody in the world into two classes — people and mugs. People include everyone who makes the legitimate economy of this country function the way it does — bankers, carpenters, scrubwomen; everyone who works for a living. Mugs are the parasites, the guys who prey on what I call 'people.' Some of them are undernourished pickpockets and some head vast illegal enterprises that bring in millions, but it makes no difference how important the mug is, or how much social position he has. A mug is a mug.'

My guest's expression had changed from puzzlement to boredom, so I cut my sermon short. 'People I let call me 'Moon,' or 'Manny,' or just 'Hey, you,' if they want. But mugs I like to call me 'Mr. Moon'.'

His bored expression disappeared to be replaced by a flared-nostril lord-of-the-manor expression. He surged to his feet, jerked his hands from his pockets and towered over my chair.

'Get on your feet, Moon,' he said curtly.

When I was twenty I decided to become heavyweight champion of the world. I only got as far as three professional bouts against tankers in the light-heavy class, all of which I won on knockouts, before the boxing commission barred me from the ring for reasons which make another story. And more mature consideration has decided me the barring did not prevent me from becoming champ, but only prevented me from becoming punchy. Nevertheless I was what the trade calls a 'steady fighter,' and I still have most of my co-ordination.

I got on my feet and let him have a left hook he didn't even see. He spun like a top and crouched over with his rear to me. Then I employed my aluminum foot to boot him head first into the sofa. From the sofa he rolled to the floor, glared at me groggily and shot one hand at his armpit. I let him look at the muzzle of my P-38.

My reaction to the hall door opening behind me was not as quick, however. Instead of turning, I merely glanced over my shoulder. A round-headed, bowlegged little man nearly as wide as he was high pushed the door closed behind him and

21

leaned his back against it. He, too, was dressed all in white, except for a contrasting black automatic gripped in one hairy hand.

'Take it easy, bub,' he said. 'Set your heater down real gentle.'

Stooping, I laid my gun on the carpet at my feet. I straightened at the same time my first guest came erect. He took two steps toward me, wound up his right arm, and let a roundhouse sizzle at my head.

My knees bent, pulling my head down a foot, and the tall man's fist whistled over my hair, the momentum carrying him clear around and causing him to stumble to one knee.

'Cut that!' the squat man said sharply. 'Want all the neighbors in here?'

The English lord struggled to his feet again and glowered at me savagely. Then he regained his sense of proportion along with his horsy grin. Drawing a hammerless revolver from beneath his arm, he wagged it at me friendlily.

'Mr. Moon prefers the funeral to the vacation,' he told his partner. 'We have to call him 'mister,' he says, because we aren't his social equals.'

The squat man ran flat eyes over me as though choosing the best spot for a bullet. 'In here, or do we take him for a ride?' he asked. 'Guess we could muffle it in a towel or something, couldn't we?'

I felt the hair rise along the back of my neck.

The taller gunman shook his head. 'He'd probably put up a fight and make noise. We better use the car.'

'I've decided to take the ten thousand and the vacation,' I said. 'Maybe I better pack.'

'Maybe you better shut up,' the tall man said. 'Get moving.'

Lifting his straw hat from the mantel, he dropped it over his little revolver and gestured with the hat toward the door. His short friend glanced at him admiringly and tried his own hat over his gun. But the automatic was too large, so he thrust it in a side pocket instead and kept his hand on it. Then he courteously held the door for me.

We met no one in the hall, nor on the half-flight of stairs to the street entrance. But

23

no more had we reached the sidewalk than a long black Cadillac convertible swooped around the corner and skidded to a stop in the 'no parking' space directly in front of the apartment. Two people were in the car, and my heart skipped a beat when I saw the driver was Grace Lawson.

At the same moment she saw me and waved gaily, the squat man whispered hoarsely, 'Geez! It's the kid! What we do now?'

'We lose the pot,' the tall man said quickly. 'Scram, and fast!'

Immediately both turned and headed down the street side-by-side at a fast walk. I stared after them with my mouth open until they rounded the corner and disappeared from sight.

I approached the car and said to Grace, 'Were you in the Girl Marines?'

'No,' she said, startled. 'I wasn't old enough. Why?'

'Because you're so prompt. Early, aren't you?'

'A little. Arnold makes me get everywhere early.' She turned her eyes to the skinny lad of twenty-two or twenty-three who sat next to her, and her tone changed to the one radio announcers use when they say, 'Ladies and gentlemen, the President of the United States.' But what she said was, 'This is my fiancé, Arnold Tate, Mr. Moon.'

As we shook hands I examined him in an effort to discover what he had that gave rich and beautiful girls the blind staggers. He seemed to possess none of the traditional great-lover attributes. No bulging muscles, no Grecian profile, no silken lashes, or golden curls. His frame was big-boned but skinny, his face long and narrow, with very black eyes, an aquiline nose, and a thin but prominent jaw. His black hair was straight and possibly had been combed, but riding with the top down had spilled it all over his forehead. He had a firm handclasp and looked like a nice guy.

I said, 'How are you, Arnold?' which he recognized as a rhetorical question, for instead of answering, he asked me the same thing.

'I was just walking to the street with some callers who dropped in,' I told

Grace. 'Be back soon as I get my bag.'

My P-38 still lay in the middle of the front-room floor. I hid it under my arm, got my grip from the bedroom, and returned to the car.

3

Grace drove as though she were rushing to a hospital and was afraid she would have a baby before she got there. She was a good driver, but the only times we got under fifty were at stop signs and red lights.

I was conscious of some sort of strain between her and Arnold Tate. During the first mile of our eight-mile drive to Willow Dale neither said a word, Arnold sitting still and aloof, as though he heartily disapproved of both of us, and our beautiful chauffeur occasionally casting appealing sidewise glances at him. Abruptly Arnold started the conversation.

'I want you to know I don't approve of this at all, Mr. Moon,' he announced.

'Of what?' I inquired.

'This subterfuge. It's ridiculous, when Grace's life is in danger, to consider anything so inconsequential as unfavorable publicity. I think the police should have been called long ago.'

'So do I,' I said.

He flashed me a surprised glance. 'Then why didn't you recommend that procedure to Grace?'

'I did.'

'Now, Arnold,' Grace broke in. 'Let's not go all over that again. Mr. Moon is a professional bodyguard and knows all about keeping people from getting killed. Don't you, Mr. Moon?'

'No. I only know how to try. The last woman I was hired to protect managed to get killed anyway.'

For a moment there was silence.

'If it'll make you feel better, I caught the murderer,' I said.

This time the silence was longer. At length, I said, 'The two men in white you saw me with when you drove up weren't exactly friends. They were professional gunmen come to warn me out of town.'

Both of them looked at me sharply.

'They seemed to know you, too, which is why they departed so quickly. But if they are the ones trying to kill you, I don't know why they didn't take this opportunity. They had me covered, and they could easily have taken over your car, forced you to drive somewhere lonely, and rubbed all three of us out.'

Grace had paled, but Arnold only looked angry. 'How did they know Grace had engaged you?' he asked.

'That's the question I intended to ask you two. Who knew she was going to?'

'No one but the two of us and Fausta Moreni,' Arnold stated with certainty, then glanced quickly at Grace.

She shook her head. 'I didn't tell anyone.'

'You can rule Fausta out,' I said. 'She chatters, but she doesn't talk. She wouldn't pass on anything told her in confidence to her own mother. That's why so many people tell her their troubles. If neither of you let it out, the only answer is that someone's been tailing Grace.'

Arnold started to twist in his seat.

'Never mind,' I said. 'I've been watching and there's no tail on us now.'

Arnold said loudly, 'I'm going to call the police the minute we get to the house!'

'You do,' Grace threatened, 'and I'll

never speak to you again.'

'Haw!' Arnold snorted. He turned to me. 'Understand, Mr. Moon, I'm not objecting to your being engaged. As a matter of fact, I think a professional bodyguard is an excellent idea. But I think it's absurd not to call the police, or for you to attempt to pass yourself off as anything but a bodyguard. If you'll pardon my frankness, you don't look like a graduate student in English literature.'

I grinned at him. 'What do I look like?'

'A prizefighter or a stevedore or an army first sergeant.'

'You win first prize,' I said. 'I've been all three.'

Grace flicked her eyes curiously at my face.

'The nose and the bum eyelid aren't from the ring,' I told her. 'I picked them up in stevedore days.'

As we neared Willow Dale, Grace pulled over to the side of the road and stopped. 'Now promise you'll behave, Arnold,' she said. 'I don't want you spoiling the weekend by exciting everybody at home.'

'I'm going to phone the police.'

She chewed her lip petulantly. Suddenly she smiled, threw the car in gear, and started again. 'Go right ahead,' she said in a deliberately sweet voice. 'I'll tell them you're crazy and I don't know a thing about it.'

For a few moments he examined her in silence, half-exasperated and half-amused. Then he shrugged resignedly. 'She would,' he told me wryly, and did not speak again the rest of the trip.

Willow Dale is not a suburb, but a section of the city. Sometimes it is called 'the millionaires' subdivision,' for the five richest families in town live there. It consists of about fifteen acres perched atop a high bluff over the river. Private gates lead into each of the five estates, and the Lawson gate was the middle one.

The sun cast its slanting glow over perfectly kept lawns as we rolled up the graveled drive. We passed a badminton court, a tennis court, and a concrete swimming pool. We couldn't see the house until we were nearly upon it, for between it and the swimming pool was a screen of weeping willows. It appeared suddenly as we passed the weeping willows, a two-story brick mansion which must have contained twenty rooms.

Grace swung behind the house and pulled into the only vacancy in a four-car garage. Two other cars were parked in the court next to the garage, and beyond the court was a small stable.

'Uncle Doug and Abigail,' Grace remarked after glancing at the cars on the court.

As I followed Grace and Arnold to a side door, I glanced over the outside of the house. It was of modern but not modernistic construction. It sat about thirty yards from the river bluff, which was edged with an iron handrail to prevent strollers from falling a hundred feet to the rocky beach below. An opening in the rail directly behind the house indicated steps descending to the beach. Beyond that I had time before we rounded the corner of the house only to observe that apartments of some kind were situated over the garage, probably servants' quarters.

Grace turned me over to an elderly house-keeper with a rawhide complexion, a mouth like a catfish, and a faint mustache.

'This is Mr. Moon, Maggie,' she told the woman. 'He's a friend of Mr. Tate's from school. Give him the room next to mine.'

My first impression of the old woman was of unbending snobbery. Her critical eye took in the cut of my clothes, the shine of my shoes, and estimated the cost of my wristwatch in a single glance. When her eyes returned to my face, her expression indicated she had reached no decision.

I am not much of a hand with young ladies, but old ones flock to me like flies to candy. I let one eyelid droop solemnly, and was rewarded by a twinkle deep within Maggie's frosty eyes. She turned abruptly and said in a soft but carrying voice, 'Kate!' Immediately a uniformed maid appeared from another room. 'Show this gentleman the fourth guest room,' Maggie instructed the girl.

As I followed Kate up the stairs, I could not help noticing the excellent legs attached to her trim, straight body. And when she opened the door to my room and stood aside for me to enter, I noted she was just as decorative from the front. She had a nice figure and fine black hair, but the prettiness of her features was somewhat spoiled by the sullen cast of her mouth. I guessed her to be about twenty.

'The bath is over there,' she said, pointing across the room. 'If you want anything, pull the cord over the bed.'

'What time's dinner?' I asked.

'Seven-thirty, but they're all having cocktails in the drawing room now, so you can go down whenever you want.'

There was an elusive air of resentment in her tone, and a deliberate absence of 'sirs.' Not that I care even if housemaids call me 'Bub,' but it struck a peculiar note in a household seemingly run like a hotel. Apparently she had a grudge, but it could hardly be a personal one against me, for I had never seen her before. I let it go by thanking her for her trouble, unpacked my small grip, and descended to the drawing room.

Grace and Arnold had not yet come down, but five other people were in the room. The first things to register on me were an evening gown and a white mess jacket, and momentarily I thought, without much concern, that my light tan gabardine suit was going to be distinctly out of place. Then I realized only two of the group were dressed, which put me with the majority.

A woman about thirty or a little over, whom I judged to be the stepmother, Ann, commanded all my immediate attention. She was as breathtakingly beautiful as Grace, but in an entirely different way. She was tall and raven-haired, with a milk-white complexion and calm, luminous eyes a man could have drowned in. She wore a dinner gown cut to look as if it were going to slip loose and slither down around her ankles at any minute, but instead of thinking it daring, you immediately accepted the fact that unnecessary concealment of such an obviously fine form would have been censorship of art.

The only other woman was a gaunt, middle-aged spinster whose uncurled gray hair was worn in a boyish bob. She had on a severely tailored gray suit and an expression like a ferret's.

Two men stood before the small bar with the ladies, one about sixty years old and the other about forty. The older man was constructed like a slab of granite, huge and solid and ponderous of movement. His face was firm and unwrinkled, except for two deep creases between his eyes, and its sculpturing was along the line of Benito Mussolini's. He wore a light blue business suit.

The other man was slight and quick-moving, a debonair man-about-town in white mess jacket and patent leather pumps. He had the sharp, amusing face of a master of ceremonies in a burlesque house.

The fifth person was a black houseboy behind the bar.

Ann Lawson glanced over at me without surprise, set down her glass, and approached with a warm smile. 'I'm Mrs. Lawson,' she said, offering me a remarkably strong hand.

I told her my name and that I had come

out at the invitation of her stepdaughter and Arnold Tate. She introduced the other woman as her aunt, Abigail Stoltz, adding the identification, 'The painter, you know,' at which I nodded agreeably, though the name meant nothing to me. The older man turned out to be Jonathan Mannering, the family lawyer, and the other Dr. Douglas Lawson, Mrs. Lawson's brother-in-law and Grace's Uncle Doug.

When introductions were completed, Ann asked, 'Are you connected with the university, Mr. Moon?'

I said no and was saved from elaboration by the entrance of Grace and Arnold. Apparently everyone suited individual taste in dinner dress here, for Grace wore a frilly, informal party dress and Arnold the same sport coat and slacks he arrived in.

'You've met everyone, have you, Mr. Moon?' Grace inquired. 'Hello, everybody. Hi, Unc!' The last greeting she emphasized by standing on tiptoes and planting a kiss on the debonair doctor's cheek.

He grinned at his niece fondly and winked at Arnold. Mrs. Lawson gave

Arnold as warm a welcome as she had me, but Mannering and Abigail Stoltz greeted him with tepid politeness.

'What will you have to drink, Mr. Moon?' Ann Lawson inquired. 'And you, Arnold?'

I said I would have rye and water, and Arnold chose a Martini. Grace settled for a nonalcoholic Coke.

Conversation stayed on a small-talk level while we worked toward the bottoms of our glasses. Amid dead silence on the parts of Arnold and myself, Grace built me an elaborate academic background, sketching in a mythical past career as a high school teacher, presumably to account for the nearly ten years I had on her fiancé, explaining that I taught in the wintertime and attended the university each summer, placing me in the same thesis seminar as Arnold, and even giving a title for my supposed thesis: *The Use of the Comma in Shakespeare*. Later I learned she had rummaged through the stacks of the university library and obtained the title from an actual master's thesis submitted ten years before.

'How'd Shakespeare use the comma?' Uncle Doug asked.

'As punctuation,' I said shortly, wishing Grace would shut her beautiful little trap.

Maggie, the housekeeper, appeared in the arch from the dining room and announced dinner was ready. During dinner I took the opportunity to study the group more closely, adding little to my knowledge except that Abigail Stoltz rarely opened her mouth, Jonathan Mannering had an old-world manner and a stock of complimentary clichés which he ponderously showered on his hostess, and Dr. Douglas Lawson had a delightful sense of humor. Ann seemed to be as fond of Douglas as her niece was, and once or twice I seemed to detect more than a sister-in-law's indulgence in her laughter at his dry wit.

We were served by Kate and the house-boy who had been tending bar. Throughout the meal I had been wondering where the fifth habitual weekend guest was, the man Grace had mentioned as general manager of the Lawson Drug chain. As we returned to the drawing room for coffee, Ann cleared up the mystery.

'Gerald Cushing will be out later this evening,' she told Jonathan Mannering. 'He wants to see you about a corporate surplus, or something important-sounding like that.'

'Indeed?' the big man intoned. 'Are you sure that isn't an excuse to visit a beautiful woman? I use business as an excuse all the time, myself.'

Which gives an idea of what the lawyer considered a delightful compliment, and is the reason I have not reported his previous conversation in detail.

I wondered if Gerald Cushing were a bachelor, too, and if he, Douglas Lawson, and Jonathan Mannering were all politely suiting for the widowed Ann's hand. My wondering was cut short by an overalled youngster about seventeen years of age, who burst in suddenly from the front porch.

'Ma'am!' he blurted out at Ann. 'There's a dead man caught on a snag halfway down the bluff!'

40

4

The initial reaction of everyone was speech-less surprise. Mine was greater than that of anyone else, for in addition to the shock of the announcement, the incongruity of a boy in overalls suddenly appearing in these sleek surroundings was startling in itself. Apparently everyone else knew who the boy was.

Ann Lawson was the first to recover. 'Where, Karl? On our property?'

He advanced further into the room, a large, gangling lad with coarse yellow hair. 'Right behind the house, ma'am. Not twenty feet from the beach stairway. You can't see him from above or below, or from the stairs, but I was out in the skiff fishin', and I seen him from the river.'

Douglas Lawson rose to his feet. 'Show us the place, Karl. How do you know he's dead?'

'He's hanging sort of head down, and he didn't move. I watched near five minutes.'

We all trooped out behind Karl and circled the house to the bluff at the rear. Though it was eight-thirty, the combination of long summer days and daylight savings time had pushed dusk to nine o'clock. On top of the bluff it was still quite bright, but since the steep bank faced east, the iron stairway was already in deep shadow.

We followed Karl down in single file, Dr. Lawson immediately behind the boy, then Ann, Abigail, Grace, Arnold, and Mannering, with me bringing up the rear. About fifty feet down we reached a ledge approximately six feet wide, and here a roofed and railed platform containing three wicker lawn chairs stretched a dozen feet both ways along the ledge. Beyond the platform the stairway again began its steep descent.

Karl went to the north railing and pointed to where the ledge petered out to a mere six inches when it reached a bulge in the side of the bluff. A light puff of wind brought a faint but unmistakable odor to us.

'He's just the other side of that,' the boy said. 'Want I should go over there

42

and see who it is?'

'You might fall,' Ann said.

Arnold put in slowly, 'Perhaps the proper person to investigate is Mr. Moon, since he has a semi-official connection with the police.'

Everyone but Grace glanced at me with varying degrees of surprise. She continued to stare at the narrow path, her face pinched and empty. I looked over the narrow railing at the fifty-foot drop, examined the slender foothold again, and shook my head.

'I couldn't make it,' I said.

'I been over there before,' Karl said. 'It's easy if you lean inward and feel your way.'

'It wouldn't be easy for me,' I said.

'It doesn't look dangerous,' Arnold insisted. 'I'll follow, if you want.'

'Sorry. I said I couldn't do it.'

He looked at me first with surprise, then his lips curled slightly. 'Acrophobia?'

'If it's any of your business,' I said, suddenly irritated, 'I have a false leg. I have to be able to see where I put my foot.'

He looked uncomfortable. 'Sorry. I'll go.'

Without further ado he swung over the railing, walked along the ledge until it began to narrow, then faced the wall and edged around the bulge sidewise.

'Just look and come back,' I called after him. 'Don't disturb anything.' In view of the odor there was no point in issuing first-aid instructions.

A long time seemed to drag by after he disappeared from sight, but actually it was only two or three minutes before he edged his way back again. He climbed over the rail without saying anything, his eyes averted from those of Grace.

'It's Don, isn't it?' she asked in a flat voice.

He nodded, still not looking at her. His eyes touched Ann briefly, then swung to me. 'He must have been there all along. Shouldn't we call the police?'

'I'll call them,' I said. 'There's nothing we can do here. Suppose we return to the house.'

The spirit of quiet festivity had been replaced by one of funereal silence when we again gathered in the drawing room. Ann conducted me to a phone in what had apparently been her husband's study and left me alone.

The number I called was not police headquarters, but the bachelor apartment of Inspector Warren Day, chief of Homicide. My long relationship with Day was a peculiar half-friendly, half-enemy one, but in spite of the fact that neither of us hardly ever spoke a courteous word to the other, we managed to maintain fairly effective mutual co-operation.

'Manny Moon,' I said when he came to the phone. 'Nobody answers at police headquarters, so I called you. They must have forgotten to pay the phone bill.'

'What bar you in?' he inquired.

'I'm out at the Lawson home in Willow Dale. Remember the Lawson kid who supposedly ran away last Sunday?'

'Vaguely. What about him?'

'We just found his body. He fell off the bluff and has been lying halfway down all along.'

'Well?' he said. 'There's cops on duty. Why bother me with a routine accident?'

45

'Because it may be murder, and if it is, it's going to require kid-glove handling. Some of the most important people in town are going to be suspects. I think it merits the personal attention of the chief of Homicide.'

'Blast you, Moon,' he growled. 'Why can't you find bodies in the daytime? You only work about a third of the time yourself, but you expect me to work night and day.'

'I don't care what you do,' I said. 'Send out a rookie if you want. He'll probably report it as an accident and let it go at that. But whoever comes better bring a fifty-foot rope to salvage the body.' I hung up without waiting for his reply.

When I returned to the drawing room, a short, stocky man wearing horn-rimmed glasses had been added to the group. He had a brisk, businesslike appearance, a cherubic face, and sparse blond hair parted in the middle.

'This is Mr. Cushing, Mr. Moon,' Ann introduced him. 'He arrived while you were phoning.'

He pumped my hand as though he

were really glad to meet me, then immediately turned his attention back to Ann. 'Of course, I won't stay under the circumstances,' he said. 'Is there anything I can do for you? Make funeral arrangements, for example?'

Before Ann could reply, I said, 'I'm afraid you'll have to stay until the police arrive, Mr. Cushing.'

The drug chain manager looked at me sharply. 'Why? What could they possibly want with me?'

'They'll want to see everyone who was here when Don disappeared.'

He looked surprised. 'How do *you* know that includes me?'

'Yes,' Jonathan Mannering put in somberly. 'Perhaps Gerald should stay, but it seems to me you're assuming a lot of authority for a guest.'

'Mr. Moon isn't exactly a guest,' Arnold announced. 'He's Grace's hired bodyguard. There's no point in keeping it a secret any longer. Someone has been trying to kill Grace, and apparently they succeeded with Don.'

In the shocked silence which followed,

47

Grace, who sat on the sofa next to Arnold, slipped her hand into his and regarded Ann and Douglas miserably.

'Preposterous!' rumbled Mannering.

'No,' Dr. Lawson said. 'Mr. Moon's profession is a surprise to me, but it's quite true someone has been trying to kill Grace. I've been doing a little quiet investigating myself, without any success.'

Ann said, 'Grace! Why didn't you say something, child?'

'Because — because — ' she said incoherently, then lapsed into silence.

'Because apparently the would-be killer is someone in the house,' I explained helpfully. 'Either one of you in this room or one of the servants.'

'Preposterous!' Mannering repeated.

I shrugged, fished a cigar from my pocket, and relaxed in an easy chair to await the arrival of the police.

They came without the usual announcement of sirens. I am not a cynic, but I could not help wondering if the Lawson eight or eighteen million dollars, whichever it was, had anything to do with their quiet arrival. I am morally certain if they came to investigate a body at my apartment, you could hear the sirens all over town.

Warren Day had with him his usual shadow, Lieutenant Hannegan, who was attired in the inevitable blue serge suit that looked like a police uniform without brass buttons. After he entered, the inspector stood in the doorway scrutinizing the assembly for a moment, his hands thrust into his suit pockets and his thin figure arched forward to allow his eyes to peer over thick-lensed glasses. His pointed, white-tipped nose aimed deliberately at one person after another, his belligerent expression almost dissolving into a popeyed gawk as his gaze touched Ann and Grace, but hardening to normal when it passed from them to Abigail Stoltz.

Then he suddenly swept his hat from his skinny bald head and barked, 'I'm Inspector Warren Day of Homicide!'

I brought my palms together silently in pantomime applause, and got a deep scowl for my effort.

'All right, Moon! What's going on here?'

49

'I'll show you the body,' I said. 'Bring lights and a rope?'

'We brought everything but the jail. Let's go.' Leaving Hannegan in charge of the people in the drawing room, Day followed me around to the back of the house. In the parking court was the laboratory truck, the morgue wagon, a pickup with a winch, and a squad car. Enough cops to spread a city-wide dragnet had come with the vehicles.

It had grown dark, so I borrowed a hand flash from one of the cops and led the inspector down to the midway platform. A uniformed policeman, a photographer carrying a flash camera, and a medical examiner followed us down.

'He's around the other side of that bulge,' I said, flashing my light on the six-inch foothold.

'I'll examine him when you get him up,' the medic announced, and started climbing the stairs again.

'Get out there and take some pictures,' Day told the police photographer.

'That ledge is pretty narrow,' the man said doubtfully.

'Get going!' the inspector bawled.

'You're insured, aren't you?'

The photographer looked at him dumbly, then slowly climbed the rail and approached the point it began to narrow. I could sympathize with his reluctance, for by flashlight the path seemed almost impassable. Holding the camera aloft in his right hand, he cautiously began to sidestep around the bulge.

Day turned to the cop who had accompanied us. 'Go up and start letting that rope down. He might as well attach the body while he's out there.'

'Yes, sir,' the man said gratefully, and started to run up the steps before the inspector could change his mind.

Twenty minutes later the body was on its way to the morgue, all the vehicles except the squad car had departed, and the inspector and I stood alone at the top of the bluff.

'Now let's have the dope,' he said. 'What makes you think it's murder?'

'I didn't say I thought it was murder. I said it might be. It might be suicide, too, or just an accident. But the dead kid and his sister were due to inherit half the mint if they reached twenty-one alive, and somebody's been trying to kill the sister. Maybe the same someone pushed Don over the bluff.'

'How do you mean, trying to kill the sister?'

I said, 'Things keep happening to her. Once the saddle girth on her riding-horse was cut so the saddle came off, once a flowerpot tried to brain her from an upper window, and once a glass of milk was poisoned.'

'How come she didn't call the police?'

I shrugged. 'Afraid of publicity. Her fiancé, Arnold Tate, and her Uncle Doug — that's Dr. Douglas Lawson — were the only two knew of it, aside from the girl. They figured it had to be someone in the house and decided to keep it quiet. Uncle Doug has been making like a detective, but he hasn't gotten anywhere.'

'How you know about all this?'

'Grace Lawson hired me to guard her body earlier today.'

'Then why didn't *you* inform the police?' the inspector snapped.

'I am, aren't I?'

52

'Haw!' he snorted, and turned to walk toward the house.

'That isn't all,' I said, falling in beside him. 'Whoever wants Grace dead has hired a couple of professional killers to tail her.' Briefly I recounted the scene at my apartment with the English lord and his squat companion.

He stopped and absent-mindedly shined his flash in my face. 'How do you figure them in the thing?' he asked.

'I can't so that it makes much sense,' I admitted. 'But it's possible the murderer was having Grace tailed to see if she went to the police and the tails reported in by phone periodically. When they reported her visit to me, he either knew who I was or found out in a hurry, and decided a bodyguard would put a crimp in his plans. So he told the boys either to induce me to leave town, or rub me out.'

'You sure they were connected with this affair? Maybe it was just someone with an old grudge sicked them on you.'

'To offer me ten thousand bucks?' I asked. 'Some grudge that would be. Besides, they recognized the girl, which is

53

the reason they let me go.'

'That doesn't make sense,' the inspector said. 'If they were after the girl, why didn't they grab her right there?'

'That's the question that's been bothering me,' I told him.

5

Apparently the group in the drawing room had not found the inscrutable Hannegan's presence conducive to conversation, for there was dead silence as we re-entered the house. Warren Day scowled ferociously at Abigail Stoltz and asked, 'You Mrs. Lawson?'

'Why, no,' she said in a startled voice.

'I am, Inspector,' Ann said quietly.

Day blinked at her, tried to maintain his scowl, but let it deteriorate into what was nearly a simper. Almost politely he said, 'I want to interview everyone privately, including the servants. Got a place I can do it?'

'Certainly.' She rose and led us back to the study from which I had phoned.

As Ann walked ahead of us, every line of her soft body was outlined by what little there was to her gown. Just inside the door she stopped and turned to face us. The inspector, who was following immediately behind her, slammed on the brakes so hard I nearly walked up his back. Quickly he sidled around her until the big desk separated them, and seated himself in the chair. Even in that secure position he seemed momentarily unable to conquer his psychotic fear of beautiful women.

'Long as you're already here, Mrs. Lawson . . . ' he started to mutter, then changed his mind. 'Send in your step-daughter first.'

Ann closed the door behind herself.

When Grace Lawson entered, I was impressed again by her cool loveliness. But whereas at our first meeting it had been the bubbling beauty of champagne, the shock of her brother's death had subdued it to the sparkle of still wine. She was too young to upset the inspector with her femininity, but even in his cynical eyes there was a flicker of admiration.

'Sit down, young lady,' he said with unusual gentleness.

Grace perched herself on a straight-backed chair in front of the desk and folded her hands in her lap.

'Moon, here, tells me somebody's trying to kill you. When was the first attempt?'

'Four weeks ago,' she said quietly. 'On a Sunday. Arnold and I were going riding — '

'Who's Arnold?' the inspector interrupted.

'Arnold Tate,' she said. 'My fiancé. That good-looking fellow you saw in the drawing room. He's wearing a brown sport coat.'

'Good-looking?' Day repeated. 'I must have missed him. Unless you mean that young guy whose hair wasn't combed.'

Grace sniffed disdainfully and said in a tight voice, 'When I started to swing up into the saddle, the girth broke as my full weight rested on the stirrup. Arnold and I examined it and found it had been cut so far only a thread or two had been holding it.'

'Who saddled the horse?'

'Karl.'

'Karl who?'

'Karl Thomas. The boy who — the boy who found Don. He's sort of a general handyman. Grooms the horses, services the cars, does minor repairs around the place, helps Jason, and so on.'

'Who's Jason?'

'Jason Henry, the outside man. Takes care of the grounds.'

'Listen,' the inspector said. 'All these people you mention are probably old stuff to you, but I never heard of them before. Would you mind explaining who everybody is as you go along?'

'All right,' she said contritely.

'Now where were we? Oh, yeah. Karl saddled the horse. How'd he explain the cut girth?'

'He didn't. He left the horses alone in the stable to come tell us they were ready. I hadn't changed to riding clothes yet, so it was fifteen minutes before we got to the stable. Almost anyone could have slipped out there in the meantime. Uncle Doug — he's Dr. Douglas Lawson — had been out in the skiff fishing, and he happened to come up the stairs from the beach just as Arnold and I went in the stable. He came over to say hello just as the cut in the girth had been discovered by Arnold, and we all three discussed what to do about it. At first we all thought it was just a rather stupid practical joke. Arnold was all for going up to the house and raising Cain with everyone, when Uncle Doug said in a sort of funny, shocked voice, 'Grace, I think someone tried to kill you.' It was after that we decided to keep it quiet and give Uncle Doug a chance to make a secret investigation.'

Warren Day asked, 'Who was here that Sunday?'

'Everybody. Generally we have the same group on weekends. There was Arnold. He's my fiancé. And Uncle Doug. That's Dr. Douglas Lawson — '

'Hold it!' the inspector said. 'Let's go back to your first method. You just rattle off names, and I'll stop you when I want identification.'

By dint of long and dogged questioning, during which the inspector gradually assumed a more martyred expression, he finally satisfied himself that as far as Grace knew, all of the servants, household members, or guests had opportunity, even Arnold, whom she had left alone in the drawing room while she changed to riding clothes. It was the same situation for the incident of the following Saturday night, or rather Sunday a.m. Arnold and Grace had been to a dance and returned about midnight. After both had retired to their rooms, Grace began to wonder if she had turned off the radio in the car. She went outside to the garage again to check, finding she had switched it off, after all. But as she reached the front door again, a heavy earthenware flowerpot that usually adorned a shelf immediately inside the upper hall window had sailed past her head and burst on the ground a few feet away.

'How come you went clear around the house to get in, instead of using the back door?' Day asked.

'Oh, we never use the back door,' Grace explained. 'That's Maggie's and Kate's. And the side door Maggie locks at night and keeps the key.'

'Who are Maggie and Kate?' the inspector asked wearily.

'Our combination housekeeper-cook and the maid. The three male servants have rooms over the garage, you see, but Maggie and Kate each have a room off the kitchen. Kate's only been here about six months, but Maggie was Daddy's housekeeper even in the old house downtown, since right after I was born. She sort of regards the back of the house as hers, and gets mad if anyone uses the kitchen door without her permission.'

'I see. And the same guests were here as the week before?'

'Yes, sir.'

'All right,' Day said. 'How about the third incident?'

This, it developed, left the suspects as numerous as before, which seemed to indicate the would-be killer deliberately planned his attempts at times when everyone could share equal suspicion. The previous Sunday afternoon Grace and Arnold had been playing tennis while Ann, the now deceased Don, Dr. Lawson, Abigail Stoltz, Gerald Cushing, and Jonathan Mannering sat around a lawn table at the edge of the swimming pool sipping drinks and watching the game. Edmund, the houseboy, had been bringing drinks for the group from the house, and Grace had called to him to bring her some iced milk. According to Edmund's later explanation to Dr. Lawson, he had passed on the request to Kate while he mixed at the bar the other drinks ordered. The milk was poured by Maggie and delivered by Kate to Edmund, who carried it out to the lawn table and set it down.

The tennis set finished in a blaze of action that brought all those seated at the table to their feet, and finally over to the court. With everyone's attention on the game, any one of them might have dropped poison in the milk unobserved. And since Jason and Karl had been trimming the grass around the edge of the pool, both of them had had the opportunity also. When the set ended, Arnold ran over to the table and brought back the milk and the Tom Collins he had ordered for himself. In the meantime, Grace had joined the group at the edge of the court.

As Arnold handed the milk to Grace, Dr. Lawson had sniffed and asked, 'What's that funny smell?'

Everyone tested the air, and Ann said,

'I smell something, too.'

Grace had also become conscious of a peculiar odor. Suddenly she raised the milk glass and sniffed at it, thereby foiling the poisoning attempt. The quick-thinking Dr. Lawson, realizing this might be another attempt on Grace's life, had said, 'That milk's sour. I'll get you some more,' and carried the glass off to the house. Later he had had it analyzed.

'Sounds like an awfully dumb killer,' Day remarked. 'Cuts the saddle girth too far to do any good, misses with a weapon big enough to flatten an ox, and picks a poison that stinks. Seems to be a kind of expert at inefficiency. Got any suspicions?'

'No, except it couldn't be Arnold, Ann, Uncle Doug, or Maggie.'

Day regarded her sourly. 'For the moment we won't rule anyone out. Now tell me about your brother's disappearance.'

'He just left a note saying he was leaving and disappeared. Sunday night we all went to bed, and Monday he was gone. We all thought he'd just run away, though no one knew why he should have. Of course we reported it to the police,

63

though no one was really very upset, because we had no idea . . . ' She frowned, and went on more hesitantly. 'Don is — was a rather odd boy. We were never as close as some brothers and sisters. Not that we weren't fond of each other, but he always seemed so withdrawn somehow. I don't think I ever really understood him. Arnold, Uncle Doug and I talked it over and decided possibly someone had been trying to kill him, too, and he ran away because he was scared. We supposed he'd be back in a day or two, for he hadn't taken any clothes with him except what he had on, as nearly as we could decide from examining his closet.'

'Where's the note he left?' Day asked.

'I don't know. It was addressed to Ann, so I suppose she has it.'

'Was the same group of guests here overnight?'

'All but Arnold,' she said. 'He has an eight o'clock on Monday, and my first class isn't till ten. So he always takes the bus back to school Sunday night. I drove him to the depot in time to catch the seven-fifteen.'

Grace paused for a moment, thinking. 'Uncle Doug was gone part of the night. He was called out to deliver a baby.'

'How long was he gone?' Day asked.

'I don't know. He has a private phone in his room for emergency calls, so the rest of the house won't be disturbed when he's called late at night. We all retired about ten-thirty, so it must have been after that.'

The inspector seemed to have obtained everything he wanted from Grace. 'Send Mrs. Lawson in,' he told her in dismissal.

At Ann Lawson's entrance Inspector Day tried what he seemed to think was an ingratiating smile, with the same horrible result that had occurred in the drawing room. I felt sorry for him. Every line of her body rippled when she walked, and at every ripple Day blinked.

'Please have a chair, Mrs. Lawson,' the inspector said. It was the first time in our acquaintance I'd ever heard him use the word *please*.

Seating herself in the same chair Grace had occupied, she turned her calm, luminous eyes on the inspector and waited for him to proceed.

Day cleared his throat. 'Were you aware someone was trying to kill your stepdaughter, Mrs. Lawson?'

'Not until this evening, when Arnold Tate made the disclosure.'

Carefully, but with visible discomfort, Day went over Grace's testimony concerning the poisoned milk, and Ann's version of the incident was substantially the same as her stepdaughter's.

'Of course, at the time I had no idea it was poisoned,' she explained. 'I simply accepted Douglas's statement that it was sour, and never thought about it again. I was unaware that Douglas had it analyzed, or that he had questioned the servants to learn who had handled the glass.'

'But you agree with your stepdaughter that anyone at all had opportunity to drop poison in the milk?'

'I suppose I have to. Even myself.'

Ignoring the pointed lead, the inspector switched the subject. 'Do you have the note your stepson, Don, left for you?'

'No. We all read it. I believe Aunt Abigail had it last. She's the gray-haired woman with the boyish bob.'

Day frowned. 'What did the note say? The exact words.'

'It was very short,' Ann said slowly. 'It read, 'Dear Ann, I hate going off this way, because no doubt it will make unpleasant publicity for you, but I think it the wisest course. Explain things to Grace and Uncle Doug.' I may not have the exact wording, but that's the sense of it.'

For the first time Day took his eyes from her face and looked over at me. 'What's that sound like to you, Moon?'

'A red herring,' I said promptly.

'What do you mean?'

'You expected me to say it sounds like a suicide note, didn't you?'

'Why, it does!' Ann exclaimed incredulously. 'That never occurred to any of us, but it could very well be, couldn't it?' She paused, then said softly, 'I should have known all along.'

'Why?' Day asked.

Ann's expression indicated she wished she had not made the remark. 'I didn't really mean that,' she said reluctantly. 'There is no reason Don should have committed suicide. It's just that he was such a moody boy . . . ' Her voice trailed off, then renewed its strength. 'It isn't fair of me to say such things, for it would never have occurred to me Don might commit suicide. He was a strange boy, and somewhat withdrawn, but certainly not pathological.'

'How about that red-herring crack?' Day said to me.

I said, 'When two kids are heirs to as much green stuff as Don and Grace, and you *know* someone is trying to knock off one, you can almost bet when the other dies violently, it was murder. Any suicide notes left lying around were probably planted by the murderer. Bet you never find that note, now that it's fulfilled its purpose.'

The inspector turned back to Ann. 'You say the note ended, 'Explain things to Grace and Uncle Doug.' What did that mean?'

'I have no idea,' Ann said. 'We all puzzled over it, but the best answer we could arrive at was that he meant for me to break the news gently to them that he had run away from home.'

'Humph,' Day remarked. Then he added, 'Send in your Aunt Abigail when you go out, will you please?'

6

The inspector's treatment of Abigail Stoltz was more in line with his usual manner. 'Sit down!' he barked as soon as she entered the door; and when she hurried to comply, he shot at her, 'Your name?'

'Abigail Stoltz,' she whispered. 'Miss.'

One after another, Day hammered questions at her concerning her occupation, her private life, her reason for visiting her niece every weekend, and a dozen other inconsequential matters. The net return in usable information was zero, and finally he ran down. Having reduced the woman to the verge of tears, eventually he asked the only question for which he had called her in in the first place.

'This note young Lawson left for his stepmother. She says you had it last. What'd you do with it?'

'Gave it to Douglas,' she said. 'Dr. Lawson, that is.'

Day swung his gaze from her face to

mine. I shrugged. 'Send in Dr. Lawson,' he ordered Abigail Stoltz.

When Douglas Lawson came in, he seated himself easily without awaiting the inspector's invitation. Day regarded him over the top of his glasses and said, 'We're trying to track down the note your nephew left behind, Doctor. Miss Stoltz says she gave it to you.'

'That's right,' he admitted. 'Have it right here in my wallet.' He fished in a leather case from his inside breast pocket and produced a folded half-sheet of stationery. Warren Day shot a look of gloating triumph in my direction. After giving the paper a cursory examination, he tossed it to me. The note was written in ink on what seemed to be half a sheet of legal-sized typing paper. It read:

Dear Ann,
I hate to leave this way, because undoubtedly the publicity will be unpleasant for you, but I think it the wisest course. Explain things to Grace, Uncle Doug

There was no signature.

'Not quite what Mrs. Lawson said, but close,' I remarked, and handed it back to the inspector.

'You sure your nephew wrote this?' Day asked.

The doctor looked surprised. 'Why, of course. It's in his handwriting.' He regarded Day curiously. 'I suppose a handwriting expert could establish it definitely.'

The inspector grunted, referred to the note, and asked, 'Any idea what the boy meant about explaining things to you and his sister?'

Dr. Lawson shook his head. 'We all discussed that at the time, but it didn't make sense to anyone. However, since we found Don's body, I've been thinking it over, and it occurs to me possibly this was a suicide note. Suicide would explain the note's apparent lack of sense, for suicides are seldom very coherent. Possibly Don's use of the word 'explain' was merely a poor word choice. As we originally interpreted the note, we all thought he was asking Ann to explain to Grace and me why he was running away, which of course she didn't know. But if you regard it as a suicide note, perhaps all he meant was he wanted her to break the news gently.'

The inspector's expression was dubious. 'Know of any possible motive for suicide?'

'Well . . . ' Dr. Lawson seemed slightly embarrassed. 'A suicide doesn't necessarily have to have what you or I would consider a motive, Inspector. The condition of his mind is motive enough.'

'But Mrs. Lawson stated very definitely that in her opinion young Don was not pathological.'

'Pathological?' The doctor looked puzzled. Then he grinned. 'Ann's — Mrs. Lawson's — knowledge of psychiatry is at best sketchy. Apparently she meant neurotic. And I'm afraid I have to disagree with my sister-in-law. Don definitely had a neurotic personality, and I was even planning to refer him to a psychiatrist for treatment.'

Warren Day's eyes lighted with interest. 'What was his trouble?'

The doctor shrugged. 'I'm not a psychiatrist. I do know enough, however, to recognize a neurotic when I see one. Among other things, Don was a hypochondriac. For the past year he has called at my office on the average of once a week with everything from tuberculosis to a brain tumor, but I've never been able to find the slightest thing wrong with him physically. He had always been a moody boy, but recently his fits of depression began to alarm me. I have to admit that the possibility of suicide never occurred to me, for if it had I would have referred him to a psychiatrist immediately. I did fear a possible mental breakdown, however; and while I would not have diagnosed Don as a potential suicide, it is not particularly surprising he became one.'

This masterful bit of post-mortem diagnosis seemed to satisfy the inspector, but left me with the mental resolve that if I ever started clawing the wallpaper, the first doctor I would stay away from was Dr. Douglas Lawson.

Day folded the suicide note and stuck it in his inside coat pocket. 'Now about the attempted poisoning, Doctor. Understand you had the milk analyzed.'

'Yes. It contained enough paraldehyde to kill several people.'

'Paraldehyde?' I asked, surprised. 'Isn't that a peculiar drug to use as a poison?'

Dr. Lawson looked at me quizzically. 'You're familiar with it?'

'Only vaguely. Had an alcoholic client once who took it to make pink elephants disappear. The guy had a suicide complex, and it was my job to see he didn't knock himself off on one of his periodic binges. I asked the doc who prescribed the paraldehyde if an overdose could be fatal, and he said it might be, but he doubted that anyone could hold enough on his stomach to kill himself, because too much makes people throw up.'

The doctor's expression was the tolerant one of a professional explaining the technicalities of his profession to a layman. 'Probably your client took it in water. Undisguised, it has a rather nauseating taste, but in milk a person could easily hold down a fatal dose. I think you'd find it listed as a poison in the Pharmacopoeia.'

'What difference does it make whether it would have killed her or not?' Warren Day interjected irritably. 'It was obviously intended to, which makes it attempted murder. Where could a person get this stuff, Doctor?'

Douglas Lawson shrugged. 'Any drug-store. You'd have to have a prescription, but anyone can obtain a prescription for a hypnotic by visiting a doctor and claiming insomnia. My own theory is that whoever is trying to kill Grace did just that, and was unlucky enough to have the doctor prescribe a hypnotic with a strong odor. The potential killer could hardly ask the doctor to prescribe a specific drug, and probably figured an overdose of any sleeping potion would do the trick.'

The inspector said, 'As I understand it, everyone in the house now was also present on each of the occasions attempts were made on your niece's life.' The doctor nodded. 'And Sunday night, when Don disappeared, everyone but Arnold Tate was here.'

'Depends on what time he disappeared,' Dr. Lawson said. 'He bade all of

76

us good night and went to his room when the rest of us retired. If he disappeared before one a.m., we were all in the house. I received an emergency call about ten of one, and left in my car ten minutes later. I didn't get back until seven-thirty, after the servants were up.'

'What was the call?' Day asked.

'A delivery. I had been expecting it, but hoped the mother would pick a more agreeable time.' He grinned. 'That's a forlorn hope, for they all seem to prefer the middle of the night.'

'Give me the details,' Day said, producing a dog-eared notebook and an automatic pencil.

'The patient was Mrs. Anna Wright,' the doctor said, spelling the last name and waiting while Day wrote it down. 'When her husband phoned, I told him to get her to the hospital, phoned the hospital to make arrangements, then dressed and drove there myself. I arrived at one-twenty, about a minute before the expectant mother.'

'What hospital?' the inspector asked.

'Millard.'

'And you were there until seven-thirty?'

'Until about seven. Ordinarily deliveries don't take so long, but this was a breach presentation, and the mother went into shock from loss of blood. I stayed to check on the intravenous until I was sure she was out of danger. The baby lived. A six-pound girl.'

'One last question,' Warren Day said. 'Why didn't you report these murder attempts to the police?'

'I suppose I should have,' the doctor admitted. 'But it seemed so certainly the work of someone in the house, I hoped I could discover who it was and turn him or her over to the police quietly, instead of getting everyone upset knowing a potential killer was loose among us.'

'Humph!' Day snorted. 'All right, Doctor. Send in young Arnold Tate.'

Neither Arnold Tate nor Gerald Cushing, who followed him, was able to offer any information we did not already have. Day made short work of them and then called Jonathan Mannering.

Mannering was able to shed no light on either Don's death or Grace's danger, but he did clear up a question which had been bothering me — whether the Lawson estate was worth eight or eighteen million, but only after Warren Day bluntly informed him he considered the will the most probable motive for the attempts on Grace's life. He meant to know its provisions even if he had to drag Mannering into court that night, and I had explained that we already knew the general provisions, and named them.

'I suppose the actual amounts involved aren't particularly important, since you seem to know everything else,' he said. 'The bulk of the estate, which was scheduled to fall to Grace and Don equally after all other bequests, a few special trust funds, and taxes are taken out, amounts to controlling interest in Lawson Drugs, with a rough market value of eighteen million dollars and about two million in cash and other convertible assets.'

'Wow!' I said. 'Twenty million bucks. Twenty million motives for murder!'

Jonathan Mannering eyed me coldly. 'Since Ann — Mrs. Lawson — is the heir in event of the children's deaths, you're implying she's the guilty person.'

'Not necessarily,' I told him. 'Maybe she's on the killer's list, too. Who's her heir?'

A curious expression of fear touched the lawyer's eyes. 'Why — why, Abigail Stoltz. But Ann really has little to leave, since the trust fund furnishing her income reverts to the Lawson estate on her death.' He paused while a look of incredulity formed on his face. 'Of course if Grace died suddenly, and then Ann died before she changed her present will, Abigail would inherit everything.' He thought a moment and added, 'No doubt in such circumstances Douglas Lawson, or other relatives of the bequestor, could break the will, or at least partially break it, since it is obvious Donald Lawson's will never intended anything to go to Abigail Stoltz. I'll have to speak to Ann about it.'

'Don't speak to anyone but Ann,' I suggested. 'Just possibly that would hurry along some murders.'

Day glanced at his watch. 'Nearly midnight. Tell Mrs. Lawson I want the servants now, but the rest of you may go to bed if you wish. And send Lieutenant Hannegan in for a minute.'

When Hannegan opened the door, Day barked at him, 'Find out where Don Lawson's room was and get some samples of his handwriting. That's all.'

'Yes, sir,' Hannegan said, and closed the door quietly.

I grinned at the inspector. 'Bet the boys at Homicide all pitch in to buy you a Christmas present each year.'

About five minutes passed before there was a knock, and the door opened without awaiting invitation. With one hand still on the knob, Maggie, the housekeeper, stood stiffly in the doorway, surveying Warren Day's bald head distastefully. The inspector examined her mustache with equal distaste. 'Well, come in and close the door!' he said testily.

Ignoring him, Maggie addressed herself to me. 'Sir, Miss Ann wants to know if these police persons would like sandwiches and coffee before they talk to the rest of us.' Her tone made it obvious she still considered me a guest, whereas the police were in the same category as tradespeople and delivery boys.

'They'd like it very much, Maggie,' I said solemnly. 'And so would I.'

'Most everyone has gone up to bed,' Maggie said. 'Will the drawing room be all right, sir?'

'Fine,' I said. 'And would you have Edmund take something to the driver out back?'

'Yes, sir. It'll be ready in about five minutes.'

'Humph!' Day snorted as Maggie departed, leaving the door open.

'Maggie is blood-conscious,' I explained to him. 'One of the old family-retainer type, who can recognize aristocracy at a glance, and has no use for the proletariat. I've mentioned those ready-made suits you wear before, and — '

'Shut up!' Day bawled. He surged to his feet and flounced out of the room ahead of me.

The only people in the drawing room were Grace and Ann, the others apparently having wasted no time in taking advantage of the inspector's permission to retire. Grace's youthful face was drawn with strain and fatigue.

'You going to bed soon?' I asked her. She nodded tiredly. 'Then I'll start earning my fee,' I said. 'I want to check your bedroom for safety.'

She nodded mechanically, bade her stepmother a tepid good night, and moved toward the stairs. I followed her up them and along the upper hallway, which was dimly lighted by a single wall lamp, to the door just this side of my own.

As she reached for the knob, I touched her shoulder and said, 'Huh-uh. As long as you're paying for a bodyguard, let's give you your money's worth. According to Emily Post, the bodyguard always goes first.'

Gently I opened the door, and felt for the wall switch with my left hand.

'Grace?' inquired a low voice from the darkness.

My left hand found the wall switch at the same moment my right found the P-38 under my arm. I aimed the latter in the general direction of the voice before flipping the former. A soft, pink glow flooded the room, disclosing Arnold Tate resting comfortably beneath a thin sheet on one of the two pillows of the double bed in the room.

I put my gun away and said gravely, 'Good evening, Arnold.'

7

Flinging back the sheet, Arnold sprang from the bed and stood glaring at me in all the splendor of orange pajamas with purple stripes.

'What do you want here?' he asked indignantly.

'Took the words right out of my mouth,' I said.

Behind me Grace giggled. Glancing over my shoulder, I saw she was staring fixedly at her fiancé's garish pajamas. Amusement struggled with the strain and grief in her face.

No man enjoys being laughed at by his ladylove. Scooping a maroon robe from the foot of the bed, Arnold shrugged it on and padded barefoot toward the door. There he turned to me, pointedly ignoring Grace.

'For your information,' he said coldly, 'this is not what it seems. With a murderer abroad, I merely felt Grace would be safer if not left alone all night.'

Grace's shoulders began to shake with laughter, and she collapsed against her defender's chest. Arnold held himself rigid, his face scarlet with embarrassment.

I said, 'Mighty chivalrous of you, Arnold. Gives me an idea.'

I crossed to the large window, glanced out, and saw it led onto a balcony. A hand grasped my shoulder and swung me around.

'What did that crack mean, Mr. Moon?' Arnold demanded.

'Relax,' I said. 'I'm not intending to steal your plan. Does your bedroom window let out on a balcony?'

'No.'

'Good,' I said. 'Climb back in bed. You can spend the night here.'

Arnold looked flustered, and Grace's giggling shut off suddenly. She studied me warily.

'And you'll sleep in Arnold's room,' I told her. 'Get your stuff and let's go.'

Arnold's expression was a mixture of disappointment and bewilderment.

'A murderer could get in this room via

the balcony,' I explained, then added cheerfully, 'If he does, the joke's on him, because he'll kill the wrong person.'

Neither Grace nor Arnold split their sides laughing.

'Get your stuff,' I repeated to Grace.

Ten minutes later I had checked every inch of Arnold's room, which was directly across from mine.

'Lock yourself in and don't open the door till morning for anyone except me,' I told her. 'If anything at all out of the way happens, yell your head off.'

'Don't you think this is all rather unnecessary?' she asked. 'Nothing has ever happened while I was asleep.'

'I hope it's unnecessary. But it hurts my reputation when clients get killed, so be a good girl and do what I tell you. Okay?'

'All right,' she said. 'Good night.' I waited outside the door until I heard the key turn in its lock.

Downstairs I found Warren Day and Lieutenant Hannegan munching cheese sandwiches and drinking black coffee. 'Where's Mrs. Lawson?' I asked Day.

'Went for a breath of air.' The inspector gestured vaguely at the front door with his sandwich.

'Think I'll try some, too,' I said, starting for the door.

'Let her alone,' he growled. 'Can't a woman go for a walk in the dark without you homing in? Always you got to chase every woman in sight.'

'Are you jealous?' I asked.

'Jealous!' he snorted, snapping fiercely at his cheese sandwich.

I gave him a sympathetic smile and went out into the dark. There was no moon, but brilliant stars made for bare visibility; and once my eyes adjusted to the darkness, I made my way around the house without difficulty. As I expected, Ann Lawson was at the bluff's handrail, staring out over the river. But, as I had not expected, she already had a companion.

Until I neared to within fifteen feet I had thought the hazy silhouette against the slightly lighter degree of blackness beyond the bluff's edge was Ann's, so closely merged were the two of them.

Only when I heard her voice say, 'Please, dear, let's go in,' did I realize a man had his arms around her.

I stopped, not with the intention of eavesdropping, but merely because I was too startled for the moment. The silhouette grew thinner and there came the unmistakable sigh of a woman being kissed. Then a man's low chuckle was followed by Dr. Douglas Lawson's equally low voice. 'Still want to go in, darling?'

Recovering from my surprise, I could easily have either returned to the house or coughed loudly. But since everyone in the house was a suspect as the murder attempter, the opportunity to listen in on a private conversation between two of the suspects was more than my snoop-conditioned mind could resist. I remained silent and listened.

Ann's voice said, 'Please don't call me that yet, Douglas. Even if I were sure, I don't want to think about it till this is over. And it isn't fair to Don.'

'Don, hell,' Douglas said roughly. 'He's been dead over a year.'

I realized he was not referring to the

corpse of that evening, but to Ann's deceased husband, who apparently bore the same name as his son.

'Not that I'd want to hurt Don if he were still alive,' the doctor went on more gently. 'You know how close we were, and if wishing would do any good, I'd wish him alive again even though it meant losing you. But nothing on earth can bring him back, and I can't stand his ghost pushing between us.' His tone grew demanding. 'Are you still in love with a dead man?'

'It's not that, dear,' she said soothingly. 'I don't know that I ever loved him as — I mean — '

'As you love me,' he said flatly.

'No,' Ann protested. 'I meant to say, as you want me to love you. I had respect for Don, and admiration, and had he lived that would have sufficed me the rest of my life. It was a calm, sure relationship, not all fire and ice like ours. And even though he's been dead a year, I can't bear to do something of which I think he'd disapprove.'

'Dammit!' the doctor said. 'He was fifteen years older than you, and caught you at twenty-three, before you'd ever had a chance to be brought alive by a man. He had you eight years of life and one after death. What the hell does he want? Eternity?'

The silhouette broadened as Ann drew back from him. 'Don was a wonderful man,' she said coldly. 'Let's go in, please.'

As I turned to start back toward the house, Douglas Lawson's voice came to me once more. 'I know how wonderful he was,' he said exasperatedly. 'After all, he was my big brother and I knew him long before you did. He was virtually my father after Dad died. He put me through medical school, set me up in practice — you don't have to tell me how wonderful he was.' His voice took on a high note. 'But wonderful as he was, he's deader than hell now.'

Ann's reply was in a soothing tone, but I was then too far away to catch it.

Warren Day glanced at me sharply as I re-entered the drawing room. I ran a cup of coffee from the silver urn sitting on a small table, added cream, and sipped it thoughtfully.

'Well?' Day growled. 'Where's Mrs. Lawson?'

'Out by the bluff.'

'So!' He guffawed. 'Gave you the brush-off!'

'She didn't even see me,' I said. 'I told you I was just going out for the air.'

His grin faded, and he regarded me suspiciously. At that moment the door opened and Mrs. Lawson came in followed by the doctor. Day's face registered first surprise, then understanding, then vindictive enjoyment.

'Are there enough sandwiches, Inspector?' Ann asked.

'Plenty, thank you,' he said hastily.

All in the same evening I had heard Warren Day say please and thank you.

'I believe I'll go up, then,' Ann said. 'If you want to stay the night, Maggie will show you your rooms. Breakfast is at eight-fifteen.'

'We won't stay,' the inspector said. 'We'll come back again about nine in the morning. I have to ask that none of your guests or servants leave the house until we give clearance, though.'

'All right,' she said. 'Good night.'

All except Dr. Lawson told her good night. Instead he told us good night and accompanied her up the stairs. As they left the room, Day watched the dapper doctor's back broodingly, then glanced down at his own rumpled shirt. 'Hannegan!' he suddenly blared at the startled lieutenant, who sat two feet away from him. 'Start bringing in the servants.' He surged to his feet and stalked back to the library-den.

The first to appear was Maggie, who gave a repeat performance of her opinion of the inspector by standing directly before him with her hands clasped in front of her, and fixing him with glittering eyes in which there was no trace of subservience.

'Sit down,' Day rasped.

'No thanks,' Maggie said. Clearly she had no intention of staying long.

'Stand, then,' the inspector said petulantly. 'What's your name?'

'Margaret Sullivan. Better known as Maggie.'

'You're the housekeeper?'

'Yep.'

'What do you know about all this?'

'Nothin'. Will that be all, mister?'

'Listen — ' Day started to say, but I broke in.

'Mind if I ask a couple of questions, Inspector?'

Day shrugged. 'Go ahead.'

I said, 'Have a chair, Maggie, and make yourself comfortable.'

'Thanks, sir,' she said, sitting primly on the straight-back in front of the desk and snorting obliquely in Day's direction. Deep behind the surface frostiness of her eyes I imagined the hint of a twinkle.

I said, 'Maggie, you've been with the family a good many years, haven't you?'

'Nineteen,' she said promptly. 'Mr. Lawson hired me just after his missus died in childbirth, back when the family lived in the old house downtown.'

I said, 'Sometimes a housekeeper knows more about her family than the family members do.'

Maggie nodded her head shrewdly. 'I don't know about other housekeepers, Mr. Moon, but I was never exactly just a

94

servant. For ten years, until Miss Ann came along, I was the only woman in the house, and the nearest thing to a mother the kids had. Not that I ever been treated like another member of the family exactly, for Mr. Don was never one to ask hired help to sit at the same table, and my place remained in the kitchen, but I did have the care of the kids in a kind of governess-like way, you might say, and often they'd come to me about stuff they wouldn't dare mention to their father. So if you mean do I know about young Don and Grace, I dare say I always knew more about what was going on in their minds than either Mr. Don or Miss Ann. I've no doubt what you're getting at is the question of whether young Don was the type of boy would commit suicide, so I'll save time by telling you right out yes, which he did.' She clamped her jaws after this remarkable dissertation and stared at me unwaveringly.

I said, 'You're a little ahead of me, Maggie, but go on. How was he the type?'

'He just was, that's all. Understand, I wouldn't say a word against young Don for the world. A fine boy inside he was, though a bit weak and terribly impulsive, which I blame mostly on his father. A child needs love, especially one with no mother, but Grace was Mr. Don's favorite and there just wasn't enough love in him left over for his son. Nor did his own sister understand the boy, or Miss Ann, either, for that matter, though I will say she made every attempt to get on with him, and young Don thought a lot of her. A moody boy he was, and easily hurt, and inclined to do crazy things on impulse, like the time he ran away and got married. You couldn't get right inside his mind, for he was a deep one, and even me he never said a word to before he pulled that stunt.'

'But what makes you think he was suicidal?'

'I don't mean he was the type would go around thinking about it all the time, Mr. Moon. I mean he *could* have done it on impulse, if he got a nasty enough shock. Like the time his father had his marriage annulled, I saw him standing at the bluff looking down one day, and the expression on his face right scared me. For a week after that I kept my eye on him as sharp as possible, but nothing happened, so I thought it was just my fancying. But that spot was right about the one he must have finally jumped from.'

'What happened to the girl he married?' I asked.

Maggie shrugged. 'None of us but Mr. Don ever saw her. Guess the mister bought her off and sent her packing.'

I asked abruptly, 'Did you know someone was trying to kill Grace, Maggie?'

Her jaw dropped, and she gazed at me blankly.

'I guess you didn't. You'll hear about it later,' I told her. 'Any idea what could have made Don take his life?'

She nodded vigorously, but her expression was withdrawn and contemplative, her mind apparently still half on the question I had asked about Grace. 'Woman trouble again. Who's trying to kill Grace?'

'Never mind that now, Maggie. Who was the woman Don was troubled with?'

'Kate. I should have known better than to hire her in the first place, but young

Don always could get around me, the young scamp. If I'd had any idea the way it would turn out, I'd never let him talk me into it. You can't blame Kate, though, for she can't help it young Don went so bad for her, and she never gave him too much encouragement that I could see.'

'Wait a minute,' I said. 'Did Don bring Kate here?'

'That's right. Where he met her, I don't know, but she was out of work at the time and had good references, so when our other maid quit, he jumped me for the job before I could even phone the employment bureau. Plain nuts he was for her, and it's my guess he jumped off the bluff because she wouldn't have him.'

Suddenly the inspector came to life. 'Send this Kate in,' he growled at Maggie.

She sniffed, ignoring him and continuing to look at me.

I said, 'Thanks, Maggie. That's all for now. Will you send in Kate?'

'Sure, and you're welcome, Mr. Moon,' she said, rising. 'But don't you be harsh with Kate. She feels as bad about causing all this as the rest of us, and it's not her fault any more than mine. Can't expect a girl to marry a man she don't love on the off chance he'll commit suicide otherwise.'

'All right, Maggie,' I said. 'We'll be easy on her. Good night.'

'Good night, Mr. Moon.' At the door she turned and grinned acidly at Warren Day. 'Good night to you, too, Sergeant.'

8

Kate's expression was no longer sullen, but the change had not improved her appearance. She had a dazed look, and her eyes were reddened from tears.

'Your name?' Day asked sourly.

'Kate Malone, sir.' I noticed she had developed the 'sir' habit since I'd last seen her.

'Sit down, Miss Malone.'

The girl gingerly settled on the straight-backed chair in front of Day's desk.

'What were your relations with the deceased?' the inspector asked abruptly.

'Why,' she said hesitantly, 'I'm just a servant, and he was one of the family.'

The inspector waved this aside. 'Let's not beat about the bush, young lady. He got you your job here and had been chasing you fast and furious ever since you arrived. Were you lovers?'

She flushed crimson. 'I'm a nice girl, mister!'

Day seemed nonplused. 'You got any questions, Moon?' he mumbled.

'The inspector didn't mean that as it sounded, Kate. What he meant was, were you and Don Lawson planning to be married?'

'I don't know. Maybe sometime. He asked me.' Suddenly, without any change in her expression, tears began streaming down her face.

'Were you in love with him?' I asked gently.

'I don't know. Sometimes. Sometimes not. If he hadn't been such a weakling . . .' Her voice trailed off to nothing.

'Did he ever threaten suicide?' I continued.

The tears stopped and her expression became uneasy. 'Not since I've been here. Once a long time ago. I knew him before I came here, you see. We broke up once, and he said if we didn't get back together, he'd kill himself. But we didn't for a while, and he never, so I thought it was just talk.'

'Did you know he'd been married?'

She nodded bitterly. 'That's why I say

he was a weakling. He let his dad talk him out of that, and he'd of let his family talk him out of it this time, if I'd married him like he wanted.'

'Did he want you to elope?'

'Oh, no,' she said, surprised. 'I don't mean he wanted me to marry him right away. In two months he was twenty-one and got his half of the estate if he was still single. He wanted to get married right after that. But he'd of backed out as soon as his Uncle Doug and Miss Grace and Mrs. Lawson got at him about marrying beneath him — I knew him too well. And I wasn't of a mind to get mixed up in that when there wasn't a chance to win.'

I said, 'Do you think he committed suicide?'

'Of course.'

'Over you?'

'Yes,' she said quietly. 'I'm awfully sorry, but I think he did.'

'Did you know someone was trying to kill Grace Lawson?'

She shook her head slowly, wide-eyed and troubled.

'Dr. Lawson says he was called out the

night Don disappeared, and got back about seven-thirty in the morning, after the servants were up. Did you happen to see him?'

'Yes, sir. He'd forgotten a key, and I let him in.'

'Did he go right back to bed?'

'No, sir. He had early breakfast, then went up just as the others were coming down. He didn't get much sleep though, because about a half hour later they discovered the note from Don.'

'What time was that?'

'About eight-thirty. You see, we serve breakfast at eight-fifteen, and when Don didn't come down, Mrs. Lawson sent me to wake him up. He wasn't in his room, and when I told Mrs. Lawson, she went up herself and found the note. Then everybody got so excited and there was such an uproar, Dr. Lawson got up again to see what was the matter.'

'Okay, Kate,' I said. 'Anything to add, Inspector?' Warren Day shook his head.

The interviews with Karl and Edmund proved to be wasted efforts, for neither seemed to know anything at all about anything. Jason Henry, the gardener, was close to a washout, too, except for the interesting discovery that he was a staunch admirer of Kate Malone. He was a big man of about forty, thick through the body and equally thick through the head.

After he departed, I toyed with the possibility that his admiration for Kate denoted secret love, and perhaps he pushed Don Lawson over the bluff in a jealous rage. But besides being a trifle farfetched, a forged suicide note seemed out of character for a simple, earthy individual such as Jason.

'With what little we have to go on,' I said finally, 'my first guess is Dr. Douglas Lawson.'

'Why?' the inspector asked.

'Because next to Mrs. Lawson he has the best motive. Mrs. Lawson, of course, has the most obvious motive. But that's just why I don't like it. It's so obvious, she'd be a sucker to try to get away with murder.'

'All right,' the inspector said. 'What's the doctor's motive?'

I said, 'Out of twenty million dollars, his brother left him only fifty thousand. Maybe he's peeved enough to commit a couple of murders and get the rest.'

Warren Day snorted. 'He couldn't get the rest if he killed everyone in the house. Grace's heir is Mrs. Lawson, and hers is Abigail Stoltz. Of course we don't know who Abigail's is, but I'll bet my next vacation it's not Dr. Lawson.'

'That's why I like his motive,' I said. 'It isn't right out in the open for every policeman to pounce on. He could stop after two murders.' I paused, then announced, 'He's going to marry Ann Lawson.'

The inspector blinked. 'How do you know?'

I told him about the bluff-edge conversation I had overheard between the two. Day regarded me disapprovingly, but I got the impression his disapproval was not so much for my eavesdropping as it was for the news that Ann Lawson had been in the amiable doctor's arms.

'Sounds like they aren't definitely engaged,' he said with unconvincing assurance. 'He'd hardly go to the trouble of killing two people just on the off chance Mrs. Lawson might say yes.'

'It's not an off chance,' I insisted. 'I know the conversation I heard doesn't sound very passionate, but he has her hooked, all right. You can tell by a woman's tone when she's in love with a man.'

'How would you know?' he asked irritably. 'Besides, according to the testimony, Dr. Lawson was the one who first noticed the odor of the milk. If he poisoned it, he'd have kept his mouth shut.'

'Maybe he saw one of the others sniffing the air, realized the poisoning wasn't going to work, and beat the other person to the jump. And who but a doctor would have a better opportunity to obtain poison?'

'That,' he said triumphantly, 'is where your whole case falls down. Would a doctor use a poison that smells?'

'Maybe not,' I admitted. 'But let's check up on his alibi, anyway.'

'What alibi? For all we know, Don might have gone over the bluff between ten-thirty, when he was last seen, and one a.m., when the doctor claims he left.'

I said patiently, 'Maybe eventually we'll

turn something up fixing the time of death. Maybe the morgue will find he wore a watch that smashed when he fell, for example. If you phone the hospital now, you'll catch the same night supervisor who was on when the doctor delivered his baby.'

After grumbling some more, Day used the study phone to call Millard Hospital and talk to the night supervisor. He talked about five minutes, then hung up the phone. 'Alibi checks,' he said sourly.

I looked at my watch and saw it was one-thirty. 'The only guy left to interview is Hannegan,' I told the inspector. 'You can do that if you want, but I'm going to bed.'

I set my mental alarm clock for eight. This Sunday morning it was off by an hour and a half, popping me awake at six-thirty. I climbed out of bed and took my time shaving, showering, and dressing, so it was nearly seven-thirty before I finally left the room.

I was reaching for the knob of the door across from mine in order to give it a routine check, when it turned by itself from inside. The door opened, and out walked Arnold Tate, still resplendent in his purple-striped orange pajamas and his maroon robe. His hair was twisted in the kind of cowlick you only get by sleeping on it. Quickly he pulled the door shut behind him and eyed me with a mixture of belligerence and embarrassment.

'It's not what you're thinking at all, Mr. Moon. You're thinking I'm carrying on some kind of illicit love affair with Grace,' he said heatedly. 'I can see it in your face.'

'That's just the reflection of your guilty conscience,' I assured him. 'I know you were just guarding her against murderers.'

His face reddened. 'You could stand to have your mind dry-cleaned.' He padded his bare feet across the hall, and slammed the door of the room he was supposed to have slept in.

I knocked on the door he had just left, and when Grace called, 'Yes?' opened it and went in. She was still in bed, a sheet pulled up to her neck, more for decorum than insulation, for already it was beginning to get hot. Her tumbled hair formed a golden halo about her head, and she looked like a fairy princess.

I sat on the foot of her bed. 'Look, angelpuss,' I said. 'I've got a sister who was your age the last time I saw her. It's none of my business, except you bring out the paternal in me. Can't you kids wait till you're married?'

She grinned at me, unabashed. 'You caught Arnold leaving, huh? I told him he'd get caught.' When I scowled at her, the grin faded. She said, 'Don't have such an evil mind, Mr. Moon. It's not what you think at all.'

I sighed and rose. 'All right. As I said, it's none of my business anyway, except I told you not to open your door. If you want me to continue guarding your body, you'll obey orders. And Arnold Tate isn't any exception to the orders.'

'Yes, sir,' she said meekly.

'Long as you're awake, you might as well get up and keep me company. I'll wait in the hall. And stop calling me sir,' I said irritably.

'All right, Mr. Moon. I'll be ten minutes.'

Her female ten minutes proved nearly

thirty by my watch, and it was eight by the time we got downstairs. The rest of the household began drifting down shortly thereafter, and we breakfasted rather glumly in the dining room, the only conversation being Gerald Cushing's assurance to Ann that he would take care of funeral arrangements and try to have the funeral scheduled for Monday, which was the next day.

After breakfast we all gathered on the front veranda in an effort to find a cool breeze, for the day was rapidly developing into a scorcher. Here conversation remained as dead as it had at breakfast, the sole effort being a question to me by Jonathan Mannering as to whether I thought the police would allow anyone to go to church.

'You'll have to ask the inspector,' I told him. 'He'll be here at nine.'

Promptly on the hour a lone squad car deposited Warren Day in front of the house. He came up the veranda steps alone, apparently having given Hannegan a Sunday off. To me this indicated the inspector had it all figured out — or thought he had.

'Good morning,' he said, scowling at everyone but Ann Lawson, and simpering at her.

'I see you have it solved, Inspector,' I said.

He looked at me, nonplused. 'How'd you know, Moon?'

'The intelligent light in your eyes.'

Frowning, he examined my face for a trace of amusement. Finding none, he prepared to give a speech. Apparently his address was directed to all of us, but as he spoke the corners of his eyes watched Ann Lawson.

'Our handwriting expert says the deceased's note is definitely his own writing, and written under emotional strain,' Day announced. 'A psychologist we got out of bed at six this morning expresses the opinion it was a suicide note. We ordered a special autopsy last night, and there is no evidence of death being caused by anything but the fall. Experts who studied the top of the bluff found no evidence of a struggle there, and there has been no rain to obliterate traces of such a struggle had one occurred. After studying the evidence, the coroner therefore declared it a suicide, and we are closing the case.' He looked around smugly.

'How do you fit the attempts on Miss Lawson's life into that theory?' I asked.

'That's easy, Moon. Who had the best motive to kill her off?' He answered himself. 'Her brother, Don. There won't be any more attempts.'

I said slowly, 'So the would-be murderer killed himself, and now we live safely forever after, eh?'

The inspector's grin changed to a scowl. 'That's right. Anything wrong with it?'

'Just one minor point. Where do the mugs who tried to take me for a ride fit in?'

The scowl became deeper. 'A guy like you has got lots of enemies, Moon. They never had any connection with this case.'

'They knew Grace Lawson by sight,' I said patiently. 'They had tailed her to my apartment, and jumped me because they didn't want my nose in this business.'

'You mean that's what you deduced,

mastermind. Probably they were brothers of some girl you wronged and cast aside.'

I lit a cigar and kept out of the rest of the conversation, which mainly concerned the inspector's brilliance. The worst of it was that he *was* a smart cop, but he had a blind spot which made him simply shrug off any conflicting little bit of evidence that marred an otherwise perfect case. I knew he was wrong, for I had too vivid a memory of that squat gunman saying to his English-lord pal, 'Geez, it's the kid! What do we do now?'

9

After the inspector left I might as well have saved my breath insofar as trying to convince anyone the whole situation was not yet over — with the exception of Arnold Tate, who, in spite of his suspicion that I had a dirty mind, made a half-hearted suggestion that I be retained as a watchdog a few days just to be sure. Everybody was so relieved Don had not been murdered by one of them, and the attempts on Grace's life could be pinned on a dead man, that there was just no way to get past the mental block.

In spite of her shock at her brother's death, Grace herself was so heartened at no longer having to doubt any of these people, she became almost gay. The same attitude of release seemed to pervade all of them, even Ann and Douglas Lawson, who next to Arnold had shown the most concern over the girl's safety, closing their minds to the possible danger Grace might still be in. Though properly horrified by the exposé of Don's guilt, their horror was more than overbalanced by relief that none of the clique still alive was a criminal.

It began to look as though I were simply arguing to keep from losing my job, so I gave up and rather curtly inquired if someone who was not intending to go to church could take me back to my apartment.

Grace said, 'I will. Come on, Arnold. We'll run Mr. Moon uptown.'

Ten minutes later I followed Grace and Arnold into the garage containing the Cadillac convertible, pitched my overnight bag into the rear seat, and slid in next to Arnold. As Grace started the engine, a yell came from the side of the house. We all waited inquiringly, looking back over our shoulders.

Douglas Lawson entered the garage, said, 'Decided to go along for the ride,' and vaulted into the small rear seat.

To keep him company I joined him, but I got back there less athletically, by using the car door.

I noticed Arnold's back stiffen and Dr. Lawson brace his feet against the floor. Before I could figure out why, I suddenly learned. Grace backed the car up with a surge of power that nearly threw me in the front seat; swung it sharply right parallel to the garage, which hurled me against the doctor; and slammed on the brakes.

'Do you always do that?' I gasped.

'Oh, I'm sorry,' she said. 'I should have warned you.'

She started to spin the wheel left, which would have headed the car toward the drive, but the steering grip offered so little resistance her hand slipped off. Blankly she stared down at the wheel as it slowly revolved one complete cycle, stopped and began to revolve the other way.

'Ho hum,' I said, climbing out of the car. 'Brother Don came back to life and sabotaged your steering column.'

Silently the rest of them got out and stood staring at the car.

'Anyone but you drive this car?' I asked Grace. She shook her head. I eyed her contemplatively. 'Having ridden with you, I know you like speed. Presumably everyone else around here knows it, too. All you got now is a minor repair job, but if that had happened on a curve at seventy, you'd have a major funeral. Four, in fact.' I told Arnold, 'Go get Karl.'

Arnold glanced at me curiously, raised his eyes to the windows of the apartment over the garage, and yelled, 'Karl!'

After a moment the youngster's head came out one of the windows above us, and he looked down inquiringly.

'Got some overalls up there?' I asked him. He nodded his head.

'Put them on and come down. I want you to crawl under this car to look for something.'

His head disappeared and a few minutes later he appeared from the end garage, which apparently contained the stairs to the garage apartments, clad in a pair of greasy coveralls and carrying a flashlight.

'The steering wheel won't work. See if you can tell why,' I told him.

Without comment he wriggled underneath, lay there for a moment with his toes sticking up, then wriggled out again. 'Somebody used a hacksaw,' he said laconically. 'Thought I heard someone down here last night, but I looked and didn't see nothing.'

I got my grip out of the back seat. 'Guess we'll have to use a different car.'

'Wait a minute,' Arnold said. 'You aren't going anywhere. If no one else wants to hire you to protect Grace, I'll pay the bill myself.'

'You won't have to, Arnold,' Grace said quietly. Her face was pale, and her eyes held the expression of someone who had been slapped by her mother. 'Will you stay on, Mr. Moon?'

'I've been trying to all along,' I told her. 'It wasn't my idea you were out of danger.'

Our return to the house put an end to its occupants' mood of suppressed gaiety. Church plans were canceled in favor of sitting around and staring at each other covertly, as though wondering which one of them was the culprit. Even so, they all seemed unwilling to face the fact that one of them was a murderer, or at least was trying to be a murderer. Delicately they skirted the subject by discussing plans for Grace's protection, as though her enemy were some person outside their own group. I had my own plans, but saw no advantage in airing them in front of the killer, who I was reasonably certain was a member of the conference.

Surprisingly enough, Abigail Stoltz made the only intelligent suggestion during the whole conversation. 'It seems to me Grace should get away from here entirely,' she said hesitantly. 'Maybe have Mr. Moon take her off some place none of us know about, and then come back here and apply all his energy to finding out what this is all about.'

'You've been reading my mind,' I told her, 'If Grace and Mrs. Lawson agree, we'll leave right after dinner.'

This brought on a discussion which finally ended in general agreement. However, most of the group felt they personally should know where Grace was hiding out — Ann because she was the girl's stepmother, Arnold because he was her fiancé, Dr. Lawson because he seemed to fancy himself her natural protector, and Jonathan Mannering on the grounds that the family lawyer should be in on the details of any matter bearing on the welfare of one of the family. I got the impression he feared I might kidnap the girl and hold her for ransom. Only Abigail Stoltz and Gerald Cushing seemed willing to be kept in the dark.

Very bluntly I threw cold water on the first four's plans. 'Possibly one of the servants is engineering whatever is going on,' I told them. 'But if Don's death was actually murder instead of suicide, the murderer is a lot smarter than any of the servants seem. Right now I'm plugging for one of you six people being the engineer. Aside from myself and Grace, *no one* is going to know where she is.'

This shut up everybody but Grace. 'I think Arnold ought to know,' she put in timidly.

'Suppose he's the murderer?' I asked sourly.

'Oh, but Arnold couldn't be!'

'Could Mrs. Lawson?'

'Of course not!'

'Or Dr. Lawson?' I asked wearily.

'Of course not,' she said less convincingly, and her eyes moved from one to the other of the rest of them.

Suddenly both palms flew to her face, and she began to cry.

Arnold Tate jumped to his feet. 'Dammit, Grace,' he shouted at her. 'We both know how to end this thing, and I'm going to do it right now!'

Grace's tears stopped as suddenly as if a valve had been closed. The look she threw at Arnold was so frightened it was almost cowering. 'Don't, Arnold! Please don't. I'll go away with Mr. Moon, and everything will be all right.' She smiled tremulously at the rest of us. 'It hasn't anything to do with all this. Nothing at all.'

Arnold strode into the house, slamming the screen door behind him. I made a mental resolution to speak to Arnold privately at the earliest opportunity.

After dinner we called a taxi instead of taking one of the other cars, because I had no intention of returning that night. Deliberately, I left the impression I would not be back because our trip involved considerable distance, but actually I wanted some free time to do a little research at the state university.

To get to El Patio by the shortest route, we should have turned right when we left the Lawson grounds. But on the principle that over-cautiousness is smarter than carelessness, I told the taxi driver to turn left. We had not gone more than three blocks in the wrong direction when I spotted a black sedan attempting to be inconspicuous a half-block behind us.

'Union Station,' I told the cabbie.

When we reached the railroad station, I carried Grace's suitcase and my own grip through the Market Street entrance. I had lost sight of the sedan after we entered downtown traffic, and in the mob at Union Station it was impossible to tell if anyone was following us.

A check of the train schedule board showed a train due to pull out north in ten minutes. I bought a one-way and a round-trip coach to a town a hundred miles north.

Our gate was number ten. Five minutes before train time we passed through it, but instead of getting on the train immediately, I led Grace to one side and peered through the iron railings at the bank of ticket windows in the main lobby. A squat, bowlegged man in a white suit stood at the window I had just left. Even from a distance and from the back he looked remarkably like the smaller of the two gunmen who had jumped me at my apartment.

Six cars up I flashed our tickets at a conductor, and we climbed on the train. But instead of going into the coach, I left Grace standing in the vestibule with our luggage while I remained on the steps looking back at the gate. Just before the conductor shouted, 'Bo-ard!' the short man in the white suit hurried through the gate and climbed into the last car. There was no mistaking him. It was the short pal of the English lord.

Picking up our bags, I urged Grace on ahead of me through the car and on into the far vestibule. There I set down the bags, pulled open the door on the opposite side from which we had entered and tossed out our luggage. Without raising the floor platform over the steps, I dropped after the bags, then turned and held up my arms to catch Grace. The train gave a jolt and started to move just as I set her down.

'What are we doing, if you don't mind?' Grace asked.

'Taking to water,' I said.

I scanned the windows of each car as it passed. Our shadow was in the last car, seated next to the window, and looked straight at us as the car rolled by. He wore one of the most startled expressions I have ever seen.

I gave him a friendly wave.

Crossing a set of empty tracks to the next loading platform, which was for a train apparently just arrived, we mingled with the few stragglers still getting off and headed for the exit to the street. Several empty taxis were lined up at the curb. I threw our bags into the first one.

'El Patio,' I told the driver.

El Patio, billed as 'The Dining Place of Kings' ever since a deposed monarch stopped there for a sandwich while passing through town, consisted of three huge rooms insofar as the public portion of it was concerned. The center one, originally a casino when the place was a gambling-house, was about the size of a first-class hotel lobby, and somewhat resembled one in that instead of the usual chrome and Bakelite furnishings stressed by cocktail lounges, comfortable sofas in front of which stood low coffee tables were spread through the room with planned haphazardness. The sofas, being the soft type you sink so far into you have to be a contortionist to get out again, were economic traps. They were so comfortable, and the effort involved in getting up again so tremendous, it was always less trouble to order another drink than to leave. And the lowest-priced cocktail El Patio served was a dollar and a quarter.

On one side of this room was the ballroom and on the other the dining room where the ex-monarch munched his sandwich. Both were nearly as large as the cocktail lounge. Later in the evening all three would be jammed and standees would be three-deep at the bar, but at two-thirty on a Sunday afternoon the place was practically deserted.

As we passed through the cathedral-like bronze doors into the lounge, a thick-shouldered man with a skull nearly as flat as his face and a mild case of acne detached himself from the bar and approached with teeth showing in a grin.

'Hi, Sarge!' he greeted me, slamming a palm the size of a pancake griddle between my shoulder blades.

During the war Moldy Greene — whose real name was Marmaduke, but derived the nickname 'Moldy' from his acne — had been the sad sack of my outfit, one of those soldiers whose well-meaning uselessness exasperated you to the point of wanting to boot him every time he stooped over while policing the area, but for whom you developed the same sort of protective fondness a mother feels for an idiot child. With an amazing lack of judgment El Patio's former owner had hired him as a bodyguard, and Moldy proved about as efficient a civilian as he had a soldier, managing to be out at the bar when his boss was murdered in his own office. Fausta Moreni inherited Moldy along with the place, and having no use for a bodyguard, converted him to official customer greeter, a job which involved grinning at people as they walked in, after which he turned them over to the head waiter. It was a perfect job for him, for in spite of his flat nose and mild acne, he had the same sort of appeal an ugly mongrel dog possesses, and people instinctively liked him. Fausta had almost broken him of the habit of pounding those he particularly liked on the back, but as an old army buddy he regarded me as above mere customers.

I said, 'Hello, Moldy. Fausta around?'

'In the office. Come on back.'

We followed him through the deserted dining room and down a hall to an office, where we found Fausta working over the books. As we stopped in the open door she was laboriously entering figures with a desk pen too long for her, the pink tip of her tongue was pressed against her upper lip to help her concentrate, and she had a smudge of ink on her nose. As always, the sight of her dark-eyed blondeness put a lump in my throat.

'Manny!' her husky voice said. She came around the desk, grabbed my lapels, and greeted me with a short but solid kiss.

'Cut it out,' I growled. 'I got a date with me.'

Fausta's eyes narrowed at Grace, then she screwed up her nose at me, turned, and went back to her chair.

'Pooh! If Grace were really your date, you would tell me some lie about business. I do not care anyway. I am through with you.'

'I need a favor.'

Her eyes narrowed again. 'All right. We will make a trade.'

'No trade this time. It's a favor for Grace, not me. I want you to hide her out a few days.'

'Surely,' she said agreeably. 'She can stay in my apartment upstairs. No rent, except each day she stays, you will take me out one night.'

'I said no trade,' I said, exasperated. 'This is for Grace, not me.'

'Pooh! Then she can sleep in the street.' She looked calmly from me to Grace, who only grinned at her.

'All right,' I said. 'I won't argue about

it. But I'll pick the nights.'

'No you will not, my smart one. You would pick them all next year.'

'Okay,' I said, giving up.

My resistance to Fausta's bargaining was always weak, but in a sense it was sincere. There was nothing I liked more than piloting Fausta around town, but it worked like a drug, and the hang-over was not worth the momentary pleasure. It made me start wondering if it really mattered whether you or your wife had the money, and by the time I decided it really did, the break had the same effect on my nerves as suddenly taking dope from an addict.

Moldy Green said brightly, 'You got ink on your nose, Fausta.'

I turned on him and snapped, 'It looks good there.' Then more mildly I said, 'This is Grace Lawson, Moldy. Nobody gets up to see her while she's here. Got that?'

'Sure, Sarge. Nobody.' Then he asked, 'How about Fausta?'

'Except Fausta and me!' I yelled at him.

10

In spite of what I had told the family, I had not entirely eliminated the servants as suspects. Tentatively I was working on the assumption that the same person had killed Don Lawson, and of the eleven suspects presumably only Arnold Tate could not be Don's killer, since he had returned to school the Sunday night Don disappeared. It was my intention to check his alibi as a first move, so that I would either have one less suspect or an exceptionally good one.

From El Patio I had the taxi driver take me to my apartment, where I left my overnight bag and returned to the taxi again. 'Bus depot,' I told the driver.

As he started up, he glanced in the rearview mirror and kept glancing at it again every few seconds for the next two blocks.

'Listen, mister,' he said finally, 'we got a tail.'

Without turning I asked, 'What is it?'

'Yellow convertible with red upholstery. Hell of a thing to tail anyone in. Sticks out like a circus wagon in a funeral parade.'

'Just pick us up?' I asked.

'Naw. Just after we left El Patio, I guess. I remember seeing him in the rearview, but I didn't think nothing of it till I pulled away just now and he pulled out right after us from a quarter-block back. Want I should lose him?'

I said, 'No. Find a dead-end street and turn down it.'

The cabbie shrugged, bore down on the gas, and sped straight ahead for three blocks. With a squeal of tires, he suddenly swung right into a narrow street that ended fifty yards on at a board fence.

I had him turn into the first driveway, jumped out, and made the corner just as the convertible careened around it as though afraid it might lose sight of us. When the driver saw the board fence ending the street, he slammed on his brakes and sat there looking foolish while I went over to him.

I said, 'Hello, Moldy.'

'Why, hello, Sarge,' Moldy Green said.

I said coldly, 'Let me guess before you make up a story. Fausta is afraid I'll fall down and hurt myself, and you're supposed to tail along and pick me up.'

'Aw, I was just riding around. How you like my new car?'

'Just the thing for trailing people,' I told him, 'though you might have the wheels painted red.'

'Yeah, I was gonna,' he said seriously. 'But Fausta said I'd be conspicuous.'

'Look, Moldy,' I said, 'you ride back to El Patio and tell Fausta I'm a big boy now and don't need a nursemaid.'

Moldy scratched his flat head. 'Jeepers, Sarge. Fausta'll be mad. How about ditching the cab and I'll take you where you want to go?'

'No,' I said shortly. 'I got enough troubles without you. You go back to El Patio and protect Grace Lawson from murderers.'

He looked at me sadly, then shrugged his shoulders and backed the car. I stood at the corner and watched until he disappeared.

At the bus depot I learned the next bus

for the state university left in ten minutes, and purchased a round-trip ticket. Taking a seat at the rear, I idly surveyed the street while waiting for the bus to start.

Just as our driver began to cut from the curb, a yellow convertible crept alongside, and Moldy Green peered up at the windows. Almost too late he slammed on his brakes, which prevented his radiator from mashing into our side, but apparently was too sudden for the car behind him. There was a mild crash, the bus stopped and the driver and passengers all peered out at the convertible. Moldy climbed out and walked back to stare ruefully at his rear bumper, which was locked with the bumper of a black sedan.

Seeing that the damage, if any, was minor, and that the bus was not involved, the driver shifted and completed his pull into the street. But not before I caught an unnerving glimpse of the black sedan's two occupants, who had stepped out either side of the car. Both were clad in white Palm Beach and wore sailor straw hats. The driver I had last seen less than two hours before on a train headed north, and his tall companion was staring down his nose at Moldy in the condescending manner of an English lord.

If we were going to have a parade, I thought, it was just as well Marmaduke Greene was in it, for while it was unlikely he would be of any help, he was almost certain to confuse the enemy as much as he did me.

During the thirty-minute ride I could detect neither the black sedan nor the convertible trailing us, nor did I see either after we arrived. I walked the three blocks from the depot to the men's dormitory.

Arnold Tate's room, a student clerk at the desk informed me, was 210. I made my way up the stairs, knocked on the door, and a voice called, 'Spit on the floor and slide under.'

Opening the door, I found a young man of about twenty lying on one of the beds in his undershirt. He jumped to his feet embarrassedly when he saw me.

'Gee, I thought you were one of the guys, or I wouldn't have hollered that.'

I grinned at him. 'This Tate's room?' I asked.

'Yes, sir, but he's not in. I'm his roommate.'

'Manville Moon,' I said, holding out my hand.

He shook it solemnly and informed me he was Willie Gillis and a junior. 'Arnold usually gets back about eight,' he said. 'He always spends the weekend in town, you know.'

'I was afraid of that,' I said ruefully. 'I missed him last Sunday, too, and I can't wait for two more hours.'

'Last Sunday?' he said, surprised. 'I was here all evening.'

'I just phoned from the depot and the clerk said he was still in town. About nine o'clock, I think it was.'

'That was a late night for Arnold,' Willie said. 'He just barely caught the last bus, the one at two a.m., and got in about a quarter of three. Hardly could make classes the next day.' Suddenly he laughed. 'Unless you know Arnold pretty well, you don't know how funny that is. Old Early-to-bed-and-early-to-rise, I call him. He says sleep is just as important as study, and won't stay up beyond eleven

even during exam week. But take your coat off and sit down, Mr. Moon. Why you wearing a coat around in this weather?'

The real reason, of course, was that a suit coat when the temperature was near one hundred was less conspicuous than a shoulder holster hanging out where everyone could see it.

'My business requires it,' I told him truthfully. 'Thanks for the invitation, but I can't stay. Give Arnold my regards, will you?'

'Glad to,' he said agreeably.

As I reached the stairs, a bell suddenly set up an infernal clangor. Instantly the halls filled with students, who moved quickly, but without running, down the stairs. From the unexcited babble of conversation around me, I learned it had only been the dinner signal, and I suddenly became hungry.

Next to the bus depot was a hamburger stand. As my bus was not due to leave for twenty minutes, I employed the time in getting rid of my hunger.

As I stepped outside again, the first

thing I saw was a car at the curb which had not been there when I entered the hamburger stand. It was a black sedan with a squat, white-suited man in the driver's seat. The rear door hung open, and in the back sat an English lord, a wide, horsy grin on his face and his hammerless revolver in his hand.

'Get in,' invited the man in the back seat.

I glanced quickly both ways along the street, hoping the yellow convertible was still in the parade, but as usual Greene was missing at the only time he was needed. Not only that, but no other living soul was on the street at the moment.

I climbed into the car, leaving the door open.

'Pull it closed,' said the tall man. I did so.

'Put your hands on the back of the front seat.'

I put my hands on the back of the front seat.

The sedan pulled away and proceeded down the street at a sedate twenty miles an hour. With his revolver muzzle gently pressed against my ribs, the tall man reached under my arm and removed the P-38 there.

'You can sit back now,' said his lordship. He moved to the far corner, keeping his gun muzzle steadily pointed toward me, but no longer touching my side.

'How did you find me after I left your bowlegged friend at the railroad station?' I asked.

His bowlegged friend emitted a low growl, but the tall man's grin remained friendly. 'Easy, chum. Had a spotter on your apartment.' His eyes flicked at the back of his companion's head. 'You made Harry look kind of like a monkey at the railroad station, but that train stops at the west end station before leaving town, so he didn't have to ride very far. Harry can act real quick, once he catches on.'

I asked, 'How'd you pick me up on the way to the station?'

'We got a system, chum. Mr. Moon, that is.'

'Sure,' I said. 'You got a phone call from the Lawson house as soon as your employer found out we were leaving.'

'You're a bright boy. See why we have to be careful with you?'

With a casualness I was far from feeling, I asked, 'This is a kiss-off trip, is it?'

'Why, chum,' said the tall man mockingly, 'how you carry on. Harry and I wouldn't harm a hair of your pretty little head . . . unless you didn't feel like telling us where you took the kid.'

'Grace Lawson?'

'You been hiding any other kids recently?' he asked softly.

'I haven't been hiding anyone at all,' I told him. 'We got arrested for jumping off the wrong side of a train, and Grace kicked a cop in the shin. Grace is still in the clink, so if you'll just call for her at police headquarters and post a hundred-dollar bond — '

The English lord transferred his pistol to his left hand and let me have the back of his right across the mouth. I sat back and stopped talking in favor of licking the blood from my lips.

We reached the edge of town, and our

chauffeur opened up to fifty. When no one had said anything for two miles, I tried my luck again.

'Long as I won't be able to repeat it to anyone after this trip,' I said, 'who's paying you for this?'

All mockery had disappeared from the tall man's eyes, to be replaced by a hard metallic glitter. 'Life's too uncertain, chum. We could get in a wreck with a cop car, or blow a tire and turn over and me and Harry get knocked out while you stay awake.'

'Oh, sure. Or maybe my fairy god-mother will turn you into a pumpkin.'

Harry said, 'There's the road ahead, but there's a car behind us.'

I started to turn my head, but the gun suddenly jabbed my ribs. 'Eyes front, buster.' To Harry he said, 'Turn anyway. If he's following, he'll turn, too.'

Dropping his speed, Harry signaled for a left turn, braked nearly to a halt and swung into a narrow dirt road. I caught a glimpse of a sign reading *Long Pine Lumber Mill*, then dust rose about the car in a cloud as Harry jammed the brakes to the floor. Behind us I heard a car swish past down the highway. Only my window and Harry's were open, but dust billowed through them to settle on our clothes and cling to our perspiring faces. When Harry wound his window shut, I followed suit, which made the car an oven.

'Maybe if we asked someone, we could find a better road,' I suggested.

'You ain't seen nothing yet,' the tall gunman told me tolerantly. 'Six days a week tractor lugs grind this road to powder. But on Sunday there's nobody closer than seven miles.'

Apparently deciding the other car had definitely gone on, Harry shifted into low and moved ahead. Our road was little more than a dirt trail, with underbrush crowding it so closely we scratched against it on both sides in the narrower spots. The July drought had parched the road surface, after which it had been pulverized by tractors to an ankle-deep layer of dust. Even though we proceeded at a moderate speed because of holes and bumps hiding under the dust, we left

141

behind us a billowing, impenetrable screen.

For about a mile we wound through heavily underbrushed wasteland and timbered area until we came to a circular widening large enough for the car to turn around. Harry swung its nose back in the same direction from which we had come and stopped.

An opaque brown blanket pressed against the car windows, blotting out the sunlight. We sat quietly waiting for the dust cloud to settle, which it did gradually until it became a thin haze. Now we could see the underbrush each side of the road, but straight ahead suspended dust still formed a blank wall.

'Want to tell what you did with the kid?' asked the tall gunman.

'I told you,' I said.

'All right,' he said evenly. 'Get out, then.'

11

I got out of the car. The sweat running down my face felt like melted ice.

Two feet from the car was a hard-packed ridge of dirt along the edge of the road, where the tractors' lugs had not ground the surface to powder. For some reason I stepped across to this so as not to sink up to my ankles in dust, as if it made any difference whether or not a corpse had dirty shoes.

Before the tall man followed me, Harry swung open the right front door, drew his heavy automatic, and centered it on my chest. The English lord stepped across as carefully as I had, but with his white suit and white shoes he had more reason. As soon as he had satisfied himself that he was practically unsoiled, he took over the job of covering me while his companion joined us.

A pale cloud of dust still hovered around us, not enough to obscure vision, but enough to tickle your nostrils. Along the route we had come it seemed to grow thicker, probably merely because we were looking through more of it and its density accumulated, rather than because it actually was thicker. Thirty yards away it was like looking at a blank wall.

Harry said, 'It's my turn, ain't it?' and cocked his automatic.

The other man raised one eyebrow. 'This guy is mine, chum. That's the agreement — in special cases you can go out of turn. This guy slugged me.'

'Don't let him push you around, Harry,' I said. 'First thing you know he'll be making all the big kills and all you'll get is the kids and old ladies.'

'Shut up!' Harry said, his eyes cold and his heavy automatic beginning to swing upward.

I started to hunch my left shoulder with the intention of swinging, not that I had the faintest hope my fist could beat his bullet, but on the theory that almost any action is less stupid than simply standing still when someone wants to shoot you. Then the sudden sound of a motor froze all three of us.

'Hold it!' the tall man snapped at Harry.

He turned to face the thinning wall of dust, beyond which the sound of a powerful car roared nearer and nearer. But the squat man's eyes never left my face.

A car shot from the haze, I caught a flash of yellow and then it was past, leaving us engulfed in a blanket of dust. For a moment visibility sank to five feet, but it was still enough for Harry to keep me safely covered, and I knew at the slightest move he would press the trigger.

Brakes screeched as the other car stopped just beyond us. Then as the taller gunman worriedly tried to squint through the dust, another sound broke through the opaque curtain.

'Motorcycle,' said Harry, both his gun and his eyes still aimed unwaveringly at me.

After the first moment of the other car's passage, the dust settled sufficiently to allow about a ten-yard area of visibility. Suddenly through the haze appeared the most welcome sight I have ever seen — a state trooper on a motorcycle, riding slowly through the fog of dust with one foot trailing.

The tall man's hammerless revolver barked once. The slug caught the trooper in the shoulder, spinning him backward clear of the slowly moving machine, which crashed on its side in a shower of dust.

At the same moment a pistol barked from the other direction, and a bullet whispered past my forehead so close it actually singed one eyebrow. Harry's gun swung from me toward this new offense and chattered off three shots as rapidly as a machine-gun burst. Before the third shot sounded I was diving headlong past the radiator, and as both Harry and his pal began to fire furiously at their flank attacker, I skittered on hands and knees toward the prone cop, raising my own personal dust screen as I went, and nearly choking to death in it.

The cop was still alive, for he groaned just as I reached him. Jerking open the flap of his holster, I swung out his service revolver and spun toward the car, drawing back the hammer as I arched the gun. It was lucky I managed this operation all in one motion, for dimly through the haze I made out Harry standing by the open car door on the driver's side, his automatic centered between my eyes.

Our guns sounded together, but mine must have been the shade of a second before his, for the bullet whistled over my head. Mine caught his upper right arm, spinning him around so that he half-fell and half-climbed into the car. The engine was still idling, and even with a useless arm he managed somehow to start it jerkily forward.

The English lord, in the seat beside him, was trying to get a shot past the driver and through the window, which was impossible unless he sent it first through Harry's head. I got a bead on Harry's face, and it would have been like shooting a sitting bird if I had not suddenly had to fall flat in self-defense when bullets from the flank assailant began to whiz all sides of me.

The sedan picked up speed with a roar

of power and surged drunkenly down the road while I was still groveling. The sudden departure left the scene again shrouded in dust.

In an invitingly sweet voice I called, 'Gre-ene!'

'Yeah, Sarge,' he answered cautiously. 'You all right?'

I got to my feet. 'Just dandy. Come here a minute.'

His dim shape materialized from the dust cloud, and he approached with a delighted grin on his face. He stopped three feet away.

'Come a little closer,' I said.

Looking puzzled, he took one more step toward me.

I haven't timed a left hook so beautifully since my last professional fight. He sat in the dust for a full minute, shaking his head back and forth. But when he finally got to his feet again, he didn't swing back. He merely refused to speak to me.

By the time we got the motor cop to the university hospital, which was the nearest one, he was in shock from a shattered shoulder. Since Greene had stayed on his feet in the ankle-deep dust except for momentarily assuming a sitting position, he was covered only by a light film. But I had literally wallowed in the stuff. It was in my shoes, down my back, in my hair, and even in my pockets. On top of that, the temperature still hovered around ninety, and perspiration had converted a good portion of the brown dust to black mud.

The registration nurse recorded information without exhibiting a sign of curiosity. But when an orderly had wheeled the wounded man away to surgery, she directed us to a mop room containing a deep sink, apparently used for filling buckets.

'You two would ruin the public washroom,' she told us. 'Wait here a minute.'

In a few moments she returned with a bar of laundry soap, a handful of rags, and two towels.

A half hour later our clothing was still dirty, particularly mine, but at least we were again recognizable as human beings.

Moldy dignifiedly waited until I was through cleaning up before he began, still maintaining his aloof silence.

Back in the lobby we found two state troopers and the town constable waiting for us. We spent another half hour explaining things to them, with me doing all of the talking, and ended by phoning Warren Day's rooms long-distance. The constable let me talk to him.

Though it was Sunday evening and Day hated to be disturbed off duty, surprisingly he was not in a churlish mood. He was in one of his pixie moods though, and he was quite capable of asking the constable to hold us overnight if it occurred to him that would be a funny joke. Recognizing the mood, I explained what had happened without my usual needling, and asked him to vouch for us to the town constable.

'How do I know you didn't shoot the cop?' he asked.

I laughed. 'You're a card, Inspector.' Then, changing the subject: 'This tall hood definitely tried to pump me about where I had hidden Grace Lawson. And I

150

forgot to tell you there was another attempt on her life this morning. I'm afraid your theory that brother Don was pulling the attempts on Grace is full of holes.'

'I guess it is,' he admitted. 'We'll throw out a net for your two playmates. Give me their descriptions.'

I gave him an item-by-item description of both assailants, speaking slowly so that he could write it all down.

'The squat one is wounded,' I told him. 'It may be only a flesh wound, and a bandage might not show under his coat. But on the other hand, I may have gotten a bone. Have your men watch for either a guy with his right arm in a sling, or with a stiff right arm.'

'All right,' Day said. 'I'll phone this in to headquarters. Soon as you get away from there, get down to the criminal records and identification department and see if you can pick out their pictures. If they're on file, we'll put photographs in the hands of every man on the force.'

'Check,' I said, and turned the phone over to the constable.

Even after Warren Day vouched for us, we were held another half-hour until the wounded trooper regained consciousness and was declared out of danger. His evidence did little to corroborate our story, since in the dusty confusion he had no idea who had shot him, and only knew he had been chasing a yellow convertible for a traffic violation.

It was at this point that Moldy broke his reproachful silence in order to explain his part in the affair. It took the combined interviewing experience of the constable, the two state troopers, and myself to get a coherent story out of him, but we finally managed it.

Having been ordered by Fausta to watch over me, my ordering him off had not discouraged Moldy. He simply circled the block, picked me up again, and followed. How he came to realize the black sedan was also following me was not clear, and how he prevented its occupants from detecting his gaudy convertible even less clear, but somehow he managed to stick to the sedan's trail. He even showed a flash of normal intelligence by going on

152

by when the sedan turned into the mill road, but in his eagerness to swing around and come back again, he reverted to type. Two hundred yards beyond the mill road was a traffic signal at an intersection with another main highway. Moldy picked that spot to make a U-turn through a red light, causing a semi-trailer to swerve around him, which in turn drove the state trooper and his motorcycle into a ditch. The cop was chasing Moldy to give him a ticket when he ran into all the gunfire.

I think they were relieved to let us go.

Although he still professed not to understand why I had slugged him, Moldy's dignified aloofness had evaporated by that time. 'If we ever have another war, I've got the perfect secret weapon,' I told him on the way back to town. 'I'm going to give you to the other side.'

'I got you out of your scrape, didn't I?' he asked. I was forced to admit he had.

I instructed Moldy to drive to police headquarters. Together we went inside and proceeded directly to the criminal records and identification department. The night-duty clerk, a big blond cop in his early twenties, said: 'Inspector Day phoned. I've been expecting you. Let's just check those descriptions again.'

As I reeled off each item of description, he converted it to code on a couple of machine file index cards. When both cards were completed, he took them into the room where the Bertillon files were kept. In five minutes he was back with two stacks of photographs, more than a hundred photos in each stack. I tackled the file denoting men of the English lord's general description, while Moldy skimmed through pictures of short, squat and dark criminals. Greene found his man a quarter of the way through.

'Jeeze!' he said. 'This baby is quite a character!'

I took the card from his hand. It was my friend Harry, all right, both front and profile, and had been taken at San Quentin five years before. His full name was Harry Sommerfield, but he was more commonly known as Harry the Horse for reasons not explained in the file. He was wanted in New York for prison break, in Michigan for arson and homicide, and in Illinois for just homicide. The FBI also wanted him for income tax evasion.

Ten minutes later I found my man. His name was Thomas 'Dude' Garrity, and his record made Harry look like a Sunday school teacher. Apparently he had never made a graven image, but aside from that he had managed to break all of the ten commandments at least once, and to have invented a couple of new crimes Moses must have neglected to copy down.

I tossed the two cards into the blond cop's lap. 'Those are the lads,' I told him.

'Fine,' he said, then glanced at the typed notations on the backs of the cards, then whistled. 'You really picked a couple of tough ones,' he said. 'We'll get it out on the air tonight, and by morning we'll have pictures for the whole force.'

'Good,' I said. 'Leave a note for Inspector Day that I'll see him or phone him sometime tomorrow.'

12

When Greene dropped me in front of my apartment, I borrowed his army automatic and holster, since my P-38 was still in the possession of the two gunmen. Standing on the sidewalk, I checked the load by pulling back the slide. It locked open, indicating emptiness.

'You knuckle-head!' I yelled at him. 'What am I supposed to do with an empty gun?'

'Guess I forgot to reload it,' he said mildly.

Fishing in his coat pocket, he produced a full clip. I traded him for the empty and went in without even saying thanks.

Possibly I was still jittery, for I opened my apartment door with the gun in my hand and the safety off. My dramatics proved unnecessary, however, for the place was empty.

I locked the door, opened all the windows, and in a few moments the place cooled off from boiling to a mere ninety-nine. After cleaning Moldy's pistol, and having a cool shower and a warm shampoo, I went to bed.

My mental alarm clock was off in the opposite direction the next morning. I set it for eight and woke at eleven. By the time I had shaved, dressed, and fixed myself eggs and coffee, it was noon.

I wore my green gabardine, which was the next lightest suit I owned after the tan one ruined by dust, and it was tailored snug through the chest. The bulge left by the .45 under my arm left little doubt about what I carried there.

The first thing I saw as I stepped out the main entrance of the apartment house was the yellow convertible parked across the street in the shade of an elm. When Moldy saw me, he grinned like a dog wagging its tail. Resignedly I crossed the street, opened the car door, and climbed in.

'If I can't get rid of you, you may as well chauffeur me,' I said. 'How long you been waiting?'

'Since eight. Figured you wouldn't be up before then.'

'Had lunch?'

'Three sandwiches.' He pointed to the

drugstore on the corner.

'Drive me out to Willow Dale.'

We drove in silence for ten minutes before I asked, 'Didn't you tell Fausta I wanted you to let me alone?'

'Couldn't. She wasn't there.'

As I was showing Moldy which drive to turn into, he said suddenly, 'Joe, the bartender, said Fausta and that girl went off somewheres in a taxi.'

'What?' I yelled so loudly he jammed on the brakes, nearly putting me on the hood.

'Don't do that,' he said reproachfully, moving the car forward again.

As I started to open my mouth the second time, the Lawson swimming pool came into sight, and I shut off what I had meant to say when I saw the two bathing-suited figures at the water's edge. 'Stop by the pool,' I told Moldy.

When he stopped, I got out and waved him on toward the parking area behind the house. Then I crossed the short strip of lawn to stand with hands on my hips looking down at Fausta and Grace Lawson.

'She refused to stay at El Patio, Manny,' Fausta said quickly. 'I could not keep her by force, so I did the next best thing. I went along.' I shifted my gaze to Grace.

'I couldn't do it, Mr. Moon,' Grace said just as quickly. 'I got to thinking if I had to suspect my own family and my closest friends, there's not much point in living anyway. Then Don's funeral was this morning, and everyone would have wondered where I was when all the rest of the family was there. It's not Fausta's fault. I made her let me go to the funeral and come home afterward.'

I didn't say anything, because there wasn't anything to say.

Edmund the houseboy appeared around the edge of the weeping willows that screened us from the house. On a tray he carried two bottles of Coke and two glasses containing ice. As he neared, I noticed the tray also contained a shot glass of dark liquor, which I surmised to be rum, since rum and Coke is Fausta's pet drink.

'Afternoon, sir,' he said to me.

'How are you, Edmund?'

159

Mixing Fausta's drink first, Edmund handed it to her, then poured Grace's plain Coke over the ice in her glass.

I asked Grace, 'Is that boy of yours coming in tonight?'

'Arnold? He's here now. We're both so upset about this, we're going to cut for a day or two. And we couldn't go to class today anyway, on account of the funeral. Arnold's up changing into swim trunks.'

I accompanied Edmund back to the house. Arnold Tate, wearing swim trunks and carrying a towel, was coming down the stairs as I started up. 'Let's go up to your room for a minute,' I suggested.

He shrugged his lean shoulders and turned to lead me upstairs. Closing the door of his room behind us, I put my back against it. 'Sit down, Arnold,' I invited. 'I have a question for you.'

Almost as though he knew what was coming, he perched himself on the side of the bed.

'There are five servants and six relatives and friends who might be responsible for the attempts on Grace's life, Arnold. But of all of them, you're the only one with an

160

alibi for the time of Don's death — presuming he was murdered, of course. Isn't that right?' I asked.

'I assume that's a rhetorical question.'

'No. I want you to tell me your alibi.'

'You lay excellent traps, Mr. Moon,' he said levelly, 'but I happened to phone my roommate that I was cutting today and tomorrow.'

I conceded the first hole. 'Then I'll change my question. Where were you last Sunday night and early Monday morning?'

'No one asked me about it before, you know,' he said. 'I never said I went back to school that night. Everyone else said I did, and I simply failed to correct the misapprehension. That's hardly the same as lying, you know.'

I waved aside the distinction. 'According to Grace, she dropped you at the bus depot in time to catch the seven-fifteen, but you took the two a.m. That leaves nearly seven hours to explain.'

'Why?' he asked. 'Since the police say Don was a suicide, no crime was committed during those seven hours.'

I regarded him steadily. 'Maybe the police will ask the coroner to reconsider his verdict when they hear about your manufactured alibi.' I put my hand on the doorknob. 'I'll let you explain to Inspector Warren Day.'

'Hey, wait a minute,' he said. 'I didn't manufacture any alibi.'

'Tell the inspector that. Maybe he'll believe you. I don't.'

'All right,' he said slowly. 'It isn't important enough to be stubborn about. I only kept quiet to save Grace and Ann any more grief than they already had. You see, I had an appointment with Don that night, and I *know* he committed suicide.'

'You mean you saw him?'

'Of course not!' he said impatiently. 'That I *would* have told the police. And if I saw him, you think I'd have let his body lie down there in the sun for a week?'

'Take it in your own words,' I told him. 'I'm temporarily out of questions.'

His face flushed almost imperceptibly. 'That Sunday Don got me aside right after dinner, shortly before I was scheduled to leave with Grace, and asked me to meet him that night. He said he was in trouble and had to talk to me, but didn't want Grace or anyone else to know. He wanted me to go to the depot with Grace as planned, but instead of taking the bus I was to meet him at midnight at a tavern he named. They open at midnight Sundays, you know.'

I nodded to indicate I knew.

'I didn't really want to talk to him, for to be frank, I never particularly liked Don. But after all he was Grace's brother, and I felt some obligation to help him if I could. So to make a long story short, I met him as he proposed. I presume he waited until eleven, when everyone in the house would be asleep normally, then sneaked out and caught the eleven-ten local bus that goes right past the house. We had a few beers apiece in a back booth and just sat there talking until the tavern closed again at one-thirty. They only stay open for an hour and a half after midnight Sunday, you know.'

I nodded again; probably no one in town was more familiar with the opening and closing hours of taverns than I.

'Then he walked with me to the bus depot, and we talked until I got on the bus at about ten of two. That's the last I saw of him.'

'Where was this tavern?'

'Fourth and Market. I don't remember the name, but it has a neon sign saying *Bar and Grill*.'

'All right,' I said. 'What was the trouble Don was in?'

'It was all mixed up. He seemed to think everything was wrong. Partly he was bitter about his father having his marriage annulled, and said he hated the memory of his father and was still in love with the girl he married, and always would be. Then he began to talk rather wildly about marrying another girl, a domestic of some sort, I gathered, but it seemed she didn't love him, or did love him and wouldn't admit it — I couldn't quite make out which. He got awfully excited about it, but when I asked how he could be in love with both his former wife and another girl, he called me a stupid ass, then immediately apologized and dropped the subject. His whole discourse was so close

164

to incoherent, I'm making it sound much more lucid than it was, because most of the time I hadn't the faintest notion of what he was talking about.

'Then he switched to castigating himself. He let me know that if he'd had an ounce of courage, he would never have let his father break up his marriage, and if he weren't a useless heel who couldn't make his own way and had to depend on inherited money, he wouldn't have let the old man's will prevent him from marrying six months ago, instead of waiting till he was twenty-one, whatever he meant by that. He said he wasn't even a man physically, and then he asked a peculiar question. He asked me what I'd do if I discovered I had leukemia.'

Arnold paused for a moment, as though organizing his thoughts. 'I asked him what leukemia was, and he said an incurable blood disease. Then he said he didn't necessarily mean leukemia, but any incurable disease. What would I do if I knew I had only six months to live? I said I'd wait six months and die, which apparently was the wrong answer, for he became angry and called me a stupid ass again.

'But immediately he apologized the second time and began to give me what I assume he thought was an explanation for the whole performance. He had to talk to someone, he said, and he wasn't close enough to Grace to make her understand, and the only two persons he loved he didn't want to hurt. I gathered these were either his former wife and the domestic he wanted to marry, or the domestic and Ann. I never quite decided which, except that the domestic was one.

'It was at this point he began to hint at suicide. Not that he actually threatened it, but he went off on a tirade about what little he had to live for and how much better off all concerned would be if he were dead. Somewhere I've read that people who talk about suicide are not likely to commit it, so instead of trying to dissuade him, as I suspected he wanted, I got flippant and quoted poetry at him.'

Arnold flushed slightly, as though ashamed to confess he could quote poetry. 'The poem I quoted just popped into my head, but I couldn't have picked one better calculated to infuriate him.' When I made no comment, he went on reluctantly. 'It was from G. K. Chesterton's *A Ballade of Suicide.*

'The gallows in my garden, people say,
Is new and neat and adequately tall.
I tie the noose on in a knowing way
As one that knots his necktie for a ball;
But just as all the neighbors . . . on the
   wall . . .
Are drawing a long breath to shout
   'Hurray!'
The strangest whim has seized me . . .
   After all
I think I will not hang myself today.'

After a moment of silence I said, 'And that made him mad?'

'Absolutely furious. And this time when he finished calling me names, he didn't apologize. When he ran down, he assumed a politely frigid air and maintained it clear up to the time my bus pulled out. Ever since we discovered the body I've been blaming myself for not

167

talking him out of it, or at least refraining from quoting Chesterton. I keep telling myself I could have prevented his death by doing so.'

Arnold drew a deep breath and rubbed the towel across his sweating forehead. 'That's the whole story, Mr. Moon. And in deference to the feelings of Grace and Ann, I think you can see why I failed to mention it after the coroner decided it was suicide. Of course if the verdict had been homicide, I would have had to tell what I knew. Obviously Don came back home, wrote his farewell note, and jumped off the bluff sometime between two and daybreak.'

I asked slowly, 'Is this what you were about to tell yesterday when Grace sidetracked you and you slammed into the house?'

As soon as I asked the question, I knew it couldn't be. A moment later I knew I should not have asked it, for his expression changed from surprise to thoughtfulness and then to a kind of eager wariness. 'That's right,' he said.

I tried to undo the harm. 'But you said

you hadn't mentioned any of this to Grace,' I shot at him.

'Did I say that?' he asked in a surprised voice. 'You must have misunderstood me. I meant to say I didn't mention it to the police in order to prevent Grace and Ann from becoming upset over the publicity. But of course I tell Grace everything.' He grinned at me blandly.

At that moment there carried through the open window from the direction of the swimming pool the excited voice of Dr. Douglas Lawson. 'Ahoy, the house!' he shouted. *'Help! Help!'*

Then faintly we heard a splash, as though someone had dived into the pool.

13

Handicapped by a false leg and nearly ten years on Arnold, I was trailing him fifteen yards when we rounded the weeping willows that hid the pool from the house. Coming behind us, Ann Lawson and Edmund ran show position and out-of-the-money respectively.

Panting, we all gathered around the tableau at the edge of the pool. Grace Lawson, dripping water, lay on her stomach unconscious, while Dr. Lawson, in swim trunks and also dripping, knelt astride her back, administering artificial respiration. Fausta Moreni stretched on her back with her small feet dangling in the water and her empty glass, overturned, lying by her side. Near her head lay the glass used by Grace.

My first impression was that both women had started to drown and had been pulled out by Dr. Lawson. I rushed to Fausta with the intention of rolling her over and administering artificial respiration, but when I touched her body, I discovered her suit was dry. She was breathing heavily but evenly.

Without touching Fausta's glass, I sniffed at it. Then, with a thumb, I pushed up one eyelid, let it close again, and stood up from my kneeling position. I returned to the group around Grace just as the doctor stopped his rhythmic movements and rose with a puzzled frown.

'There doesn't seem to have been enough water in her to worry about,' he said. 'But she's out like a light.'

'Knockout drops,' I explained. 'In both their drinks.'

The entire group stared at me stupidly. Dr. Lawson was the first to recover. Dropping to one knee, he rolled Grace over and thumbed up an eyelid. Then he listened to her heart, felt her pulse, and rose again.

'Let's get them up to the house,' he suggested.

Returning to Fausta, I got one arm under her knees and the other behind her shoulders and began carrying her to the house. It was not the first time I had ever carried her, but now she was 115 pounds of dead weight, which makes a surprising difference. Behind me staggered Arnold, similarly carrying Grace. Dr. Lawson brought along the two empty glasses that had caused all the trouble.

Abigail Stoltz came in from the dining room as we entered the front door; her eyes grew large and she asked, 'What's the matter?'

I grunted in reply and moved on to the stairs. We deposited Grace and Fausta side by side on the bed in Grace's room. Dr. Lawson had followed us into the room and stood holding the two drinking glasses as though wondering what to do with them. His trunks were still wet enough to drip an occasional drop of water on the rug.

'Set them on the dresser,' I told the doctor.

Carefully he set the two glasses side by side, then frowned at them. 'I doubt that we'll be able to get an analysis unless they hit it on the first test,' he said. 'There's barely a drop left between the two of them.'

'Think it could be anything more poisonous than knockout drops?' I asked.

He shook his head, but his expression was worried. 'Not likely from the symptoms.' He turned toward the doorway, where Ann, Abigail Stoltz, and Edmund hovered. 'Get my bag from my room, will you, Edmund?'

A few minutes later, after employing his stethoscope on both sleeping women, checking their pulses, and again thumbing open their eyes for a moment, Dr. Lawson said, 'My guess is chloral hydrate, or what is commonly known as a Mickey Finn. The heart action is strong enough to indicate only a moderate dose, but they'll be out for a matter of hours.'

'Then nothing can be done for them now?' I asked.

He shrugged. 'Let them sleep it off. A stomach pump might bring them out of it a little sooner, but would probably leave them sicker than if we do nothing at all. I really don't think there is any danger of their having obtained a lethal dose.'

I turned to the three people standing near the doorway and said, 'I want you all down in the drawing room. And stay there until I tell you differently.'

All three looked startled, but Edmund and Abigail submissively started for the stairs at once. A flash of anger heightened Ann Lawson's beauty, and she remained where she was.

'It's another murder attempt, Mrs. Lawson,' I said more gently. 'I'm assuming charge until we can get the police here, so I'm afraid you'll have to obey my orders even though it is your house. Will you phone the police before you go in the drawing room, please?'

Her anger died to uncertainty. Finally, in a small voice, she said, 'All right,' and followed the others.

'Now just what happened?' I asked Dr. Lawson.

'I really don't know,' he said. 'I went out to the pool for a swim.' He glanced at Arnold's swim trunks. 'I suppose none of us should be swimming so soon after Don's funeral, but it's too hot for propriety. And I found Miss Moreni lying in the sun asleep, as I thought. Just as I prepared to dive in, I saw Grace down in the deep end, drifting toward the bottom. I yelled to the house for help, then jumped in and pulled her out. Judging from the small amount of water in her lungs, she must have just fallen in, and I got her out again in practically no time. I used to be a lifeguard as a kid, you see.'

'You think she fell in, then?' I asked.

His eyebrows went up. 'You mean possibly someone threw her in after she was unconscious?'

'What else?' I said. 'Whoever is trying to kill her could hardly depend on her falling in the pool when she passed out. As a matter of fact, I was present when those drinks were delivered by Edmund, and Grace sat three feet from the edge then. The position of her glass indicates she stayed right there while she drank her Coke, so she must have been thrown in.'

Dr. Lawson ground his right fist into his left palm. 'A minute earlier, and I'd have caught the killer in the act!'

'A minute later,' I said dryly, 'and you might as well not have arrived at all.'

'But what a stupid way to attempt murder!' Arnold Tate protested. 'It would have been much simpler just to poison her drink.'

I shook my head. 'I thought about that all the time we were carrying them up here, trying to figure out how the killer managed to dope the drinks. Both bottles were open when I first saw them, and I'll have to check Edmund before we can know definitely, but I imagine we'll find those bottles weren't out of his sight from the time he opened them until he delivered the drinks.'

'You mean Edmund doped them?' Arnold asked, puzzled.

'Not necessarily. In fact it's most unlikely. But since any carbonated drink goes flat if it stands too long, it isn't probable Edmund uncapped the bottles, then left them standing while he went off and did something else. I imagine we'll find uncapping the bottles was the last thing he did before picking up his tray and starting for the pool.'

Both of them continued to look at me in puzzlement.

'How many people in this house drink Coke?' I asked.

Arnold looked blank, but Dr. Lawson said slowly, 'Just Grace, I believe. She always has a Coke when the rest of us have cocktails.'

'And wouldn't everyone in the house know that?'

'I suppose so. Yes, of course they would.'

'So presumably,' I said, 'a few bottles of Coke are always in the refrigerator for Grace.'

'Very likely,' the doctor said.

'Anyone, even as inefficient a murderer as this one seems to be, could reason that out,' I went on. 'Coke in the refrigerator. No one but Grace normally drinks it. Dope *all* the Coke in the refrigerator, and who is most likely to pass out eventually?'

'Grace, of course,' Dr. Lawson said pettishly. 'Is this an exercise in juvenile logic?'

I ignored the question. 'But the killer couldn't be sure someone else might not decide to have a Coke. One of the servants perhaps, or a strange guest

177

— and as a matter of fact, a strange guest did order one. If he was just after Grace, he probably wouldn't want to chance accidentally killing half a dozen other people along with her.' I glanced at Arnold. 'That answer your question about why the drink wasn't poisoned instead of merely doped?'

'Yes,' he said doubtfully. 'But how could he know she'd be near the pool when she drank one?'

'I have no idea,' I admitted. 'For that matter, Edmund may knock my whole theory into a cocked hat by telling us he left the open bottles unattended for a while.'

Arnold was frowning at the two women on the bed. 'I have an idea,' he said slowly. 'I never thought of it before, but for a teetotaler, Grace has pretty definite drinking habits. After a horseback ride, or a tennis or badminton match, she always has iced milk. Out by the pool, and during the cocktail hour, she always orders a Coke. She was almost bound to get the dope either at the pool or at cocktails.'

I thought this over. 'That fits in neatly,' I said. 'If she gets it at cocktails, everyone is puzzled, but no real harm is done the killer. If he is lucky, she passes out alone by the pool and, screened from the house by the willows, he dumps her in the water. Except for the pure accident of a combination lifeguard and doctor arriving just after it happened, this time it would have worked. And except for Fausta being present and obviously doped, it might possibly have passed for an accidental drowning. Maybe this guy — or woman, whichever it is — isn't as inefficient as he's seemed in the past.'

Going over to the bed, I smoothed aside Fausta's bright hair and felt the pulse behind her ear. It seemed slow, but steady, and her breathing was still regular. As I looked down at her sleeping face, it occurred to me it was going to be a distinct pleasure to catch this particular killer, for the only thing in the world which could make me more determined to nail anyone who passed at one of my clients was for him to accidentally catch Fausta in the crossfire.

I asked the doctor, 'Think I should get one of the women up here to get Grace out of that wet swimsuit?'

'The bed's already wet,' he said. 'And in this heat it hardly matters.'

I turned to Arnold. 'You and Dr. Lawson stay right in this room until I get back. No one else gets in for anything. Understand?' He nodded mutely. 'And you, Doctor?'

'All right,' he said. 'Under the circumstances someone has to stay, of course.'

Downstairs I stuck my head into the drawing room and motioned to Edmund. 'Tell me, Edmund,' I said, when he had come over to the door, 'after you opened those two Coke bottles, were they out of your sight?'

'No, sir. I opened 'em just 'fore carrying 'em out.'

'Good,' I told him. 'Have you seen Mr. Greene?'

'You mean your gentleman's gen'man, sir? In the kitchen, last I saw, sir.'

I made my way back to the kitchen and found Maggie, Kate, and Moldy Greene sitting at the table drinking iced coffee.

Maggie and Kate got up when I looked in, and Moldy waved an expansive hand. 'Hi, Sarge. Draw up a glass and sit down.'

I motioned the two women back to their chairs then turned to Moldy. 'What's this gentleman's gentleman stuff?'

Greene looked puzzled and Maggie's face suddenly assumed a suspicious frown. 'Isn't this gentleman your valet, sir?' she asked.

'No,' I told her.

'Well!' she said in an outraged voice, 'he came to the kitchen door and said he was with you, so naturally I assumed he was your gentleman's gentleman.'

I crooked my finger at Moldy, who was staring at Maggie in astonishment. When he came over to the door, I pushed him through it in the direction of the stairway.

'He's not a guest, either, Maggie,' I said ever my shoulder. 'I bought him from a circus for a pet.'

I led my moronic friend upstairs, directed him into the room where Fausta and Grace lay, and gestured toward the bed. Ignoring Grace entirely, he stared down at Fausta in bewilderment.

'What's the matter with her?' he asked.

'Knockout drops,' I said.

Knotting both oversized fists, he glared at Dr. Lawson and Arnold belligerently. 'Who done it?'

'We don't know yet,' I told him. 'I'm going to give you a simple task even you won't be able to ball up. See that chair?' I pointed to a cushioned straight-back near the window. 'Sit in it and stay there until both Fausta and Grace wake up. Dr. Lawson and I are allowed in the room. If anyone else tries to get in, pitch him or her out.'

'Out the window?' he asked interestedly.

'Out the door!' I yelled. 'Just keep everyone else out.'

'How about me?' asked Arnold.

'No,' I said. 'It would be too much of a strain for him to remember three people. Just the doctor and me.'

We left Moldy in charge. Arnold and the doctor went to their rooms to dress, while I returned to the kitchen. Maggie, now alone, examined me with suspicion when I stuck my head in the door.

Apparently I had fallen in her estimation because of my association with Greene.

'There's been another accident, Maggie,' I said. 'Heard about it?'

Her eyes spread, and an expression of alarm displaced the suspicion. 'Not Miss Grace?'

'Yes, but nothing serious. She's all right now. Any Coke in the refrigerator?'

'Well, yes. Some. Four bottles, I think.'

'Get it for me, will you? All of it.'

After a moment of curious scrutiny, she went to the huge refrigerator in one corner and brought out four bottles of Coke. 'Do you want them opened?' she asked politely.

'No.'

Setting the bottles on the table, I held one level with my eyes and carefully examined the cap. Then, holding the bottle with both hands, I pressed my thumbs upward. For a moment nothing happened, then with a slight pop, the cap flew off.

'Why, that's the strongest thing I ever saw!' Maggie exclaimed.

I grinned at her. 'It's a trick, Maggie. Someone uncapped the bottles, then pressed the caps back on.'

Recovering the loose cap, I snapped it back in place. 'How long have these been cooling?'

Her brow furrowed. 'How long? I don't know. Three, four days maybe. When they get low, I put in a dozen, so I guess it's been three days at least since I added any.'

I thanked her and departed with the four bottles.

14

Upstairs I set the Coke bottles on Grace's dresser next to the two empty glasses. 'These aren't to drink,' I told Moldy. 'They're full of knockout drops. Don't let anyone touch them till the cops arrive. Think you can remember that?'

'Sure,' he said resentfully. 'Think I'm a Mormon?'

'While you were in the kitchen with Maggie and Kate,' I said, 'did either of them leave at any time?'

'Not Maggie, but Kate did. The young one, you know. She hadda set the dining room table, and was gone about fifteen minutes, I guess.'

'Did you leave yourself?'

'Me? No. Why should I set the dining room table?'

By the time I finally got to the drawing room, where I had sent Ann, Abigail Stoltz, and Edmund to wait for me, Arnold and Dr. Lawson had completed dressing and were also there. As I entered the room from the hall, I caught a glimpse of Kate through the archway into the dining room. She was doing something at the table, and getting a sudden inspiration, I crossed to the archway to observe what it was. She was laying silver on the bare tablecloth, and apparently she had just started. 'Kate,' I said.

She turned quickly. 'Yes, sir?'

'Come in here a minute. I want you in on this.'

Kate approached diffidently, and I could not help marking the change in her manner since our first contact. Her subdued air of resentment had been replaced by one almost of shyness, as though she were prepared to run at the drop of a hat.

I turned to Mrs. Lawson. 'Did you phone the police?'

'Yes,' she said. She was pale, but composed.

'If nobody objects, I'd like to ask a few questions before the police arrive,' I said.

Nobody seemed to have any objections.

'For the benefit of those who don't know what's going on,' I said, 'someone slipped a drug in Grace's Coke, then tossed her in the swimming pool unconscious. Assuming it was the same person who made the previous murder attempts, the field is now considerably narrowed. We can eliminate Arnold Tate because I was with him at the time Grace was attacked, and we can eliminate Dr. Lawson because he was the one who saved her life. Jonathan Mannering and Gerald Cushing are out because they weren't here — '

'Pardon me,' Ann interrupted softly. 'Jonathan stopped in before lunch to have me sign a paper. He stayed for lunch and left only about ten minutes before Douglas's yell brought us all out of the house.'

After I thought this over, I said, 'So we can eliminate Gerald Cushing, anyway. That leaves Mrs. Lawson, Miss Stoltz, and Mr. Mannering among the relative-and-friend group. Of the five servants, Maggie has an alibi for the time, which leaves four. If any of you can verify where you were just before Dr. Lawson yelled, please speak up.'

No one said anything. 'Mrs. Lawson?' I asked.

'I was in my room, but I'm afraid no one saw me after Jonathan left.'

'Miss Stoltz?'

'Lying down,' she said apologetically.

'Edmund?'

'Part-time in here, sir. Part-time in th' kitchen. But I wouldn't throw Miss Grace in no pool.'

'Kate?'

For some reason her face had turned pale. 'In the dining room,' she said almost inaudibly.

'Doing what?'

'I was supposed to be setting the table,' she said, her eyes on my shoes.

'But it still isn't set,' I told her gently. 'What were you doing?'

'Crying,' she said simply.

I studied her face for a moment, started to ask, 'About what?' then changed my mind because I thought I knew. 'Get Jason and Karl,' I told Edmund.

He disappeared in the direction of the kitchen. Hardly had he gone through the door when footsteps sounded on the veranda and the door chime rang. I crossed and answered it myself.

'*Well?*' Inspector Warren Day growled.

I stepped aside and he entered. Behind him came the granite-faced Jonathan Mannering, looking more like Mussolini than ever; and behind him was the inspector's satellite, Hannegan.

Day glowered at Abigail Stoltz, simpered at Ann Lawson, then barked, 'Afternoon!'

'Good afternoon, Inspector,' they all chorused back like a classroom greeting its teacher.

I said to Hannegan, 'Know Marmaduke Greene at El Patio? The guy they call Moldy?'

Hannegan nodded, never being one to employ one word where none would do.

'You'll find him third door to the right upstairs. He's guarding two unconscious women, two empty glasses, and four bottles of Coke. The glasses and Cokes are for analysis, with chloral hydrate suspected.'

The lieutenant raised an inquiring eyebrow at Day. 'All right,' the inspector said irritably.

As Hannegan started toward the stairs,

Day said to me, 'What's going on here? Something new happen?'

I told him about the attempted drowning.

'Phone in about it yet?'

'Mrs. Lawson did,' I said, surprised. 'Aren't you here in response to the phone call?'

'No. Was on my way out anyway, because of what happened yesterday. Suppose half the division will show up now.'

He glowered around the room and suddenly boomed, 'All right! I want everyone together here who was present when this last incident took place.' He turned to Kate. 'Round up the servants.'

'Just get Maggie,' I told her, then explained to the inspector, 'I sent Edmund after the other two just before you and Hannegan arrived.'

Day grunted. 'Were you here then?' he shot at Mannering.

'Why — no — I mean, I don't know,' the lawyer said. 'Not when Dr. Lawson called out, certainly. But I must have been gone only a few minutes.' To Ann he explained, 'I met the inspector on the road about a mile from here, and he waved me down.'

'Took you a long time to drive a mile, didn't it?' I asked.

Mannering turned toward me stiffly. 'It's a hot day,' he said frigidly. 'I stopped for an ice-cream soda.'

Maggie and Kate came in, followed by Jason Henry, Karl Thomas, and Edmund.

'This everyone in the house?' Day asked Ann Lawson.

She nodded. 'Except that man with Mr. Moon and Miss Moreni.'

'If you don't mind, Inspector,' Arnold Tate put in, 'I'd like to make an announcement before you begin asking questions.'

The inspector examined him sourly. 'Go ahead.'

'I don't know who is trying to kill Grace,' Arnold began slowly, 'nor why, but I can visualize a number of possible reasons. Ann, as Grace's heir, may be doing these things — '

'See here!' Dr. Lawson interrupted angrily.

'Or Miss Stoltz, as Ann's heir,' the young man went on imperturbably, 'may plan to kill both Grace and Ann. Mr. Mannering, as executor of the estate, may have some motive less obvious than these. Or Mr. Cushing may have mismanaged the corporation's funds in some manner.' He glanced at the inspector. 'We don't have to stick only to those here now, you know. The Coke could have been doped yesterday, and perhaps Cushing was hiding near the pool awaiting an opportunity.' Arnold turned from the inspector to Dr. Lawson.

'Even you, Uncle Doug, might appear to have the motive of making Ann rich and then marrying her, except we both know you could accomplish that without murder if you really wanted to — make Ann rich, I mean; not marry her. And besides, you saved Grace's life.'

'Is this supposed to be an announcement?' the inspector asked impatiently.

'No, Inspector. Just give me a minute, please.' Speculatively Arnold ran his eyes over the five servants. 'What motive any of you could have, I don't know. But it is at least conceivable one of you believes you can somehow gain by Grace's death. My own opinion is that somehow or other the will is tied up in all this, so I want to straighten out a misapprehension in the murderer's mind.' Deliberately, Arnold rested his eyes on the face of each person present, one after another. 'Whoever you are, murderer, Grace's life means more to me than twenty million dollars. You may stop trying to kill her now, because she isn't heir to the Lawson estate.' He paused, then said distinctly, 'Grace and I have been secretly married for nearly six months.'

'Arnold!' Ann Lawson cried.

'You shouldn't have done that, Arnold,' Dr. Lawson said quietly. 'Ann knew it, because I told her, and I don't see how it could possibly mean anything to anyone else.'

'See here, Ann!' Jonathan Mannering put in. 'Do I understand both you and Dr. Lawson knew this all along?'

'Yes,' Ann said simply.

'But this changes everything!' the lawyer exploded. 'With young Don dead,

193

and Grace married, you automatically become heir. Why on earth did you keep it silent?'

'Just a minute!' Inspector Day roared. 'Let me ask the questions here.' He peered over his glasses at Ann. 'All right, Mrs. Lawson. Mind telling me what you're talking about?'

Ann looked about ready to cry at any minute. 'You see, Inspector, I never approved of the marriage clause in my husband's will. Of course, with Grace being so young, had I known she planned to marry, I would have done everything in my power to dissuade her.' She glanced quickly at Arnold. 'Not that I disapprove of you, Arnold. I just feel you should both have finished school first.' Her eyes shifted to Jonathan Mannering. 'But once the deed was accomplished, I felt it unfair for Grace to lose her heritage simply because she married the man she loved. And of course up to Saturday it would merely have meant Don got everything if the secret got out. But even though it now makes me the heir, I still feel it's unfair to Grace.' She paused and looked defiantly at the lawyer. 'The money's going to Grace anyway. I won't take it from her.'

Mannering said ponderously, 'I'm afraid you have no choice, my dear. What you do with your money afterward is your own business, but there is no way I know of that you can avoid inheriting.'

'Do I understand,' Warren Day asked in a pinched voice, 'you don't want twenty million dollars?'

'It's not that exactly,' Dr. Lawson explained for her. 'Maybe you'll understand better if I tell you the whole story.'

'Do,' Day told him.

'You see,' the doctor began, 'Grace has always been a favorite of mine, and since Don died — my older brother, that is, Don Senior — I've sort of taken the place of her father insofar as advice and confidences are concerned. It was for this reason more than any other, I suppose, she told me about planning to marry Arnold. I tried to talk both of them into waiting, for, after all, Grace is still little more than a child. But when it seemed obvious they were going ahead with or without my blessing, I gave up arguing and decided to help them.' He turned faintly red. 'Matter of fact, I gave the bride away. Naturally I felt honor-bound to keep the secret —'

'Then how'd you happen to tell Mrs. Lawson?' the inspector interrupted.

The doctor's color deepened even more. 'Why — I'm in the habit of — I mean, we generally confide family affairs to each other.' He paused, smiled crookedly, and blurted out, 'Maybe I'm just henpecked. We're planning to be married one of these days.'

'Douglas!' Ann's face had turned crimson, but the light dancing in her eyes was certainly not from embarrassment.

I glanced at Jonathan Mannering's face. Suddenly he looked like an old man.

Lieutenant Hannegan strode into the room and delivered the longest speech I ever heard him make.

'That trained ape up there won't let me in the room!'

15

Warren Day asked softly, 'Would you like reinforcements, Lieutenant? A couple of squads with tear gas?'

Hannegan's face turned red. Without a word he about-faced and started upstairs again. 'Excuse me,' I said to Day, and ran after him. Catching the lieutenant at the top of the stairs, I brushed past him and reached the bedroom door first.

Moldy sat in the chair where I had left him, a twin of the automatic he had loaned me in his hand. It was at full cock, and the safety was off.

'Hi, Sarge,' he greeted. 'What d'ya think? That plain-clothes cop who's always with Warren Day tried to bust in here.'

'Put up your gun, Moldy,' I said.

'Sure,' he said obligingly, snapping on the safety and tucking it under his arm.

Crossing to the dresser, I picked up the four bottles by their necks with one hand

and picked up the glasses with the other. I delivered them to Hannegan in the doorway.

The lieutenant expelled air through his nose, made a sharp right turn, and disappeared.

'He acts mad about something,' Moldy commented.

I examined the two women, found them still breathing deeply, and returned to the drawing room.

As I entered the room, Jason, the gardener, was saying, 'I didn't see or hear nothing.'

Hannegan had set the empty glasses and Coke bottles on the bar. Just after I came into the room, Kate appeared through the dining room arch with a paper bag in her hand. She crossed and gave it to Hannegan. 'This big enough?' she asked.

The lieutenant grunted and began transferring the Coke and glasses to the bag.

Warren Day said to me, 'The gardener here says he was rolling and lining the badminton court about the time Miss

Lawson was tossed into the pool. The badminton court isn't fifty yards from the pool, but he's blind and deaf.'

'There's a hedge between the badminton and tennis courts,' Jason said sullenly.

'I know,' I said. 'One about shoulder-high. Were you working on your hands and knees?'

'Part of the time,' Jason said. 'While I was laying the chalk-line.'

'I passed there on the way in not a half-hour before Dr. Lawson yelled,' I told Day. 'Nobody was on the badminton court then.'

Jason turned belligerent. 'Maybe I hadn't started. All I know is when I pushed the roller past the pool after getting it out of the garage, Miss Grace and that other woman were sitting there. After that I never left the court till Edmund came after me.'

I asked, 'Did the two women have glasses in their hands when you saw them?'

'Never noticed. Miss Grace called hello to me and I said hello back, then went about my business. You can ask questions all day, and I won't know no more when you stop.'

I turned to Day. 'How about Karl here?'

'In the stable at the time,' Day said gloomily. 'Claims he'd been currying the three riding-horses for over an hour when Edmund found him.'

He regarded the five servants. 'All right,' he snapped. 'You can go back to work.'

Day turned his attention to Ann Lawson. 'I'd advise you to get your stepdaughter out of the house and keep her away somewhere until this is cleared up.'

'We tried to,' Ann said in her soft voice. 'Mr. Moon took her away, but she refused to stay.'

'Better try again, Moon,' Day told me. 'But another incident like this and I'll run you out of here and assign a department man to protect Miss Lawson.' He turned and strode out of the house, followed by his shadow, Hannegan. I caught them at the bottom of the veranda steps.

'Wait a minute, Inspector,' I said,

catching his arm. 'What's the score?'

'Nothing to nothing!' he snapped. 'What's the point of going around in circles asking everybody the same old questions again? No suspects, no leads.' He lowered his head to glower at me over his glasses. 'I'm going home to get drunk.' Turning his back on me, he started to walk away.

'Hold it a minute,' I urged him. 'I agree with Arnold Tate that somehow the will must be behind this mess. So let's try an oblique approach. Now, all we know about the will is what Mannering told us, and maybe he was lying. How about subpoenaing a copy and looking it over? And maybe one of our suspects is in financial straits. How about having their financial statuses investigated?'

'You mean secretly?'

'Of course. Do you need written permission from all eleven suspects?'

'As a matter of fact, we do,' he said in a ponderous tone.

'Look, Inspector,' I interrupted, 'it's me, Moon, you're talking to — not the commissioner. Don't tell me the banks and investment companies in this town won't cooperate if the cops ask for a little off-the-record information. I could get it by myself from some of the banks, if I promised not to use it in evidence. Take a few of those college cops you're always complaining the chief assigns you, have them contact the credit bureau, the various banks — '

He said coldly, 'I know how to conduct an investigation, Moon.'

'All right. Conduct one, then,' I said. 'At least we can now eliminate three suspects, which is progress of a sort, even if it is negative.'

'What three suspects?' he asked.

'Arnold Tate, Maggie, and Dr. Lawson. Tate was with me when Grace underwent this last attack, Maggie was with Moldy Greene, and the doctor pulled Grace out of the pool, so he could hardly be the one who threw her in.' I paused, then added, 'If you assume Don's killer is the same person who is passing at Grace, those three can be dropped as suspects there, too.'

'Suppose it isn't the same person?' Day growled.

'Even if it isn't, I think we may be able to eliminate Dr. Lawson and Arnold Tate. If you want to do some checking, we may be able to narrow the time of Don's death down to sometime between two-thirty a.m. and seven, when the servants got up.'

'How?'

'First,' I said, 'you'll need a good recent picture of young Don.'

Day turned to Lieutenant Hannegan. 'Go inside and get a picture,' he ordered.

As Hannegan silently re-entered the house, I went on. 'A local bus going downtown passes the house at eleven-ten at night. Find the driver who was on that night and see if Don Lawson wasn't a passenger. There is a tavern at Fourth and Market — I don't know its name, but it has a neon sign reading *Bar and Grill*. Check the bartender to see if Don wasn't there in a back booth from midnight till one-thirty, when the bar closed. Then question all the bus drivers who came this way from downtown from two a.m. on, and I think you'll be able to establish the time he got home.'

'Where'd you get this lead?'

'From Arnold Tate, but it was more or less in confidence, so I'd prefer you to hold off questioning him for the moment. If the story checks, Dr. Lawson is clear because he would have been at the hospital when Don went over the bluff. If it doesn't check, better pull Arnold in for a going-over. While you're at it, check the two a.m. university bus to see if Tate was on it. If he was, and we can prove Don Lawson was on a bus coming home about the same time, Tate will be clear on that angle, too.'

'Why would Tate be on a two a.m. bus?' Day asked querulously. 'Grace Lawson dropped him off for the seven-fifteen p.m.'

'It's a long story,' I said. 'And not important to the case unless it's a lie. I'm not holding out on you, but I'm kind of morally bound to keep Tate's confidence.'

'You'd better not hold out,' Day grumbled. 'You'll need the department's recommendation for a license renewal one of these days.'

Hannegan came out of the house carrying a cardboard-framed picture in the hand not occupied by the bag of bottles and glasses. He handed the picture to Day.

'Now go back and get a picture of Arnold Tate,' the inspector snapped. 'Try Grace Lawson's room — er, Mrs. Tate, I mean. She's bound to have a picture.'

'I'll get it,' I said quickly, remembering that Grace's room still contained Moldy Greene.

I managed to locate a picture and was handing it to Day when a car roared up the drive at a rate of speed too fast for safety. When the inspector saw white lettering on its hood, he bellowed, 'Hey!' in such an enormous voice, the driver slammed on his brakes and skidded to a halt at a point just before the drive passed alongside the building. Two uniformed officers jumped from the car and approached the veranda abreast, becoming noticeably paler the nearer they got to Warren Day.

'Glad to see you boys in such a hurry,' the inspector said in a silky voice. 'It can't be more than an hour since the call went in.'

Not having the stomach to witness two strong men reduced to groveling wrecks, I turned away and went back into the house just as the inspector's voice began to ascend to a subdued shriek.

When I re-entered the drawing room, I found Dr. Lawson and Arnold Tate had gone upstairs to check on Grace and Fausta. Abigail Stoltz and Ann Lawson were alone. 'May I speak to you privately?' I asked Ann.

'Why, yes,' she said, rising from her chair, then glancing sidewise at her aunt. 'We can go in the den.' Abigail rose, also. 'No, don't go to that trouble — I was going to my room anyway.'

Before I could reply, she hurried toward the stairway. Ann resumed her seat, and I situated myself on the sofa across from her chair.

'We're more or less at a blank wall, Mrs. Lawson,' I told her. 'This thing makes so little sense, all I can see to do is start over from the beginning. Only this time I'd like to start further back.'

'I'm afraid I don't follow.'

'I'm trying to approach the subject

delicately,' I said. 'I'd like to go back to your husband's accident.'

Ann's beautiful eyes widened. 'I don't understand what you mean, but you needn't be delicate about it. My husband died nearly a year ago, and I'm quite recovered from the shock.'

'Just a few minutes ago a thought occurred to me,' I explained. 'When your husband died, his will left everything to Don and Grace. When Don died, all the money was then due Grace, providing she lived to collect. If any one of the five attempts on Grace had been successful, you'd have inherited everything.

'Now your husband's death appeared to be an accident, and Don's appeared to be suicide. If the first attempt on Grace had succeeded, probably her death would have passed as an accident, which leads me to wonder if either your husband's or Don's death was what it seemed. Maybe this is a chain of murder, with you next on the list.'

Ann's expression changed to one of utter astonishment. 'But my husband couldn't have been murdered. It was an auto accident. The chauffeur skidded on wet pavement and went over a twenty-foot bank.'

'Was the chauffeur killed, too?' I asked.

'No.' She looked puzzled, then went on slowly, 'But if you think he might have done it deliberately, you'll have to think again. The chauffeur broke three ribs, an elbow, nearly lost an eye, and was hospitalized six weeks. Would a murderer go to all that trouble?'

'Doesn't seem likely,' I admitted. 'Anyone else injured?'

'Douglas — Dr. Lawson sprained an ankle and broke his nose. He and Donald were riding in the back seat, you see. Donald was thrown over the seat against the windshield, but Douglas only slammed forward against the front seat.' She paused, then stated quietly, 'My husband's neck was broken, and he died instantly.'

I muttered something about being sorry I had brought it up. As an afterthought, I asked what had become of the chauffeur.

'I really don't know,' Ann said. 'Since both the children and I preferred to drive ourselves, we had no use for a chauffeur after Donald was gone. Of course I kept track of him for a month or two after he got out of the hospital, but he didn't seem to need any help. He got well over a thousand dollars in addition to medical expenses from the insurance people, you see, so he wasn't in financial difficulties.'

'What was his name?'

'Vance Logan. He lived somewhere on Sixth with a married sister for a time after leaving the hospital. But I seem to remember hearing he'd moved into an apartment of his own. Possibly you'd find it in the phone book if you want to look him up.'

'He probably couldn't add anything important,' I said noncommittally. 'Let's try another angle. I know practically nothing about the background of anyone in this case. Maybe if you filled in the outlines, we might uncover a possible motive.'

'All right,' she said. 'I'm willing to help any way I can.'

'Let's start with you.'

She smiled without exhibiting any surprise. 'My parents were poor but honest. Dad was a bank teller twenty years, and died the year they made him assistant cashier. I was thirteen at the time and had four younger brothers. I passed up high school in favor of a two-year secretarial course, got a stenography job with Lawson Drugs at fifteen, and helped out the family until the last boy was through high school. By that time I was twenty-two and had worked up to Mr. Lawson's private secretary. A year later we were married.'

'A modern Cinderella,' I suggested without irony.

She flushed. 'I *did not* marry Donald for his money, if that's your implication. I never pretended even to him that I was fired with a deep and burning love, but I was fond of him and I respected him, and would have married him had he been a grocery clerk.' She eyed me with a kind of inward perplexity, then went on patiently, 'You have to understand I'd never really known any other men. Until I was twenty-two I doubt that most men ever gave me a second glance. Not that I blossomed overnight from a weed into a beautiful flower, but from fifteen on I turned in so much of my money at home, I never could afford beauty parlors and decent clothes.'

She laughed ruefully. 'I wore my hair straight back with a knot at the nape of my neck, used no make-up, and dressed in 'sensibly tailored' suits. I'm afraid I was regarded by older people as a good example and by my fellow office workers as a stick in the mud. When my youngest brother finally finished school and got a job just three months after Mom died, I suddenly discovered all the money I made was mine. But being so used to living on practically nothing, before I knew it I had saved two hundred dollars.'

A light of amused reminiscence appeared in her eyes. 'On my twenty-second birthday I went downtown and spent every cent of the two hundred on clothes and a beauty course. A week later I was private secretary to Donald.'

'An interesting history,' I told her, 'but I'm afraid I can't detect any murder motives in it. Let's go on to — say, Jonathan Mannering.'

16

'Jonathan's life has been as easy as mine was hard,' Ann said. 'Everything was planned for him even before he was born. Jonathan is the sole surviving member of the firm of Mannering, Mannering, and Mannering, the first two having been his grandfather and his father. All three attended Harvard Law School — at different times, of course — and I suppose there isn't a more trustworthy law firm in the country. Or a stuffier one. They handle no criminal cases or divorces, restricting their clientele to large corporations, though they do give legal service to families connected with the corporations retaining them. Jonathan's grandfather, who founded the firm, was probably well off, his father was considered moderately wealthy, and I suppose Jonathan himself is rich.' A half-smile lit her face at some inner thought. 'He must be, for he's been accumulating money all his life, and I've never seen him spend any.'

I said, 'He's executor for the estate, isn't he?'

'Yes, but you won't find a motive there, in case you think he may have been dipping into it. I'm sure Jonathan has all the money he could spend for the rest of his life, and he has no heirs. Then, too, though he's a bit dull, he's scrupulously honest.'

'Fair enough. How about Gerald Cushing?'

'I don't know Gerald as well as Jonathan,' Ann said. 'I've known Jonathan ever since I became Mrs. Lawson, for he and Donald were personal friends. Donald and Douglas lived in the Mannering home for six years after their parents died, you see, and came to regard Jonathan as a sort of foster uncle. But I've really only known Gerald well since Donald died. I knew him as an acquaintance, of course, for he was first vice-president of Lawson Drugs until my husband's death, after which he became president of the board of directors and at the same time assumed the position of general manager of the whole chain. I only know he came from a wealthy family, is a widower without children, and owns about ten percent of the stock in Lawson Drugs. My husband thought very highly of him.'

'Maybe he would like to own more of the stock,' I suggested.

Ann frowned. 'How could he accomplish that by murder? He isn't mentioned in the will.'

I shrugged. 'To date we haven't discovered how anyone accomplished anything by killing Don, or could by killing Grace. Now tell me about your aunt, Miss Stoltz.'

'She's a sister of my father's,' Ann said. 'I never met her until after my marriage, because she went to Paris before I was born and lived there twenty-five years. When she returned to the States about five years ago, she looked me up, decided to settle in town, and has kept an apartment at the Plaza ever since.'

'Did she ever bother to look you up when you were poor?' I asked.

'No, but she isn't like that at all. She wasn't even in this country then, you see, and my marriage to Donald had nothing to do with her return. She had become quite well known as a painter and was having an exhibition in New York. The German occupation had soured her on France, so when she got back to this country, she decided to stay. She certainly didn't look me up because she thought I had money. She visited all four of my brothers, too, and while all of them have done fairly well, none is even faintly wealthy.'

'How's it happen none of your brothers visit you on weekends?' I asked. 'Everyone else seems to use the place like a hotel.'

'They don't live here. Two are in Detroit, one in New York, and the married one lives in Chicago.'

'That explains that,' I said. 'It's been bothering me ever since you mentioned your brothers. Isn't Miss Stoltz your sole heir?'

Ann shook her head. 'Not since this morning. Because of the way Donald

215

drew up his will, I really hadn't much of my own — too little to divide among four brothers really — so I had Aunt Abigail made my beneficiary. But after you and Grace left Sunday, Jonathan pointed out that if both Grace and I died suddenly, the whole Lawson estate would fall to Aunt Abigail. He suggested I change my will with that eventuality in mind, and after some discussion I asked him to draw up a new one leaving Abigail two thousand dollars — about what she would have gotten under the original will — and the residue divided equally between my four brothers and Douglas. That's the paper Jonathan brought me to sign this morning.'

After digesting this, I asked, 'Does your aunt know of this change?'

'She was present when it was signed. I used your friend, Miss Moreni, as a witness.'

'Which doesn't leave much motive for Aunt Abigail,' I decided. 'Let's go on to Dr. Lawson.'

A faint flush suffused Ann's cheeks. 'After Douglas's public announcement, discussing him as a murder suspect is going to be somewhat embarrassing,' she said. 'I'm afraid I'm prejudiced enough in his favor to refuse even to entertain the idea he might be guilty, so I'll probably make a poor witness.' She paused to look at me frankly. 'As a matter of fact, since he told everyone we plan to be married, there's no point in hiding that I think I'm in love with him.'

'Why did you say 'think'?' I asked curiously.

'Shyness, I suppose. It's rather difficult to tell a man you don't know very well you're in love with another man. For me, anyway. Can't we talk about Arnold Tate first?'

'No,' I said. 'Let's dispose of the doctor.'

'Well,' she said reluctantly, 'Douglas was the second of three boys, and Donald was the oldest. Both their parents and the youngest son died in the influenza epidemic during World War I, when Donald was fifteen and Douglas seven. Their father carried a little insurance and owned a drugstore, so they weren't left destitute.

'Old Abel Mannering, Jonathan's father, was executor of the estate — the firm didn't restrict its clients to million-dollar corporations in those days — and had himself appointed guardian. The old Lawson house, the same one Donald and I lived in when we were first married, was rented, and the two boys moved into the Mannering home.

'Two years later Donald graduated from high school and went to work in the drugstore. The store hired a registered pharmacist who was also supposed to be its manager, but apparently he wasn't a very forceful man, for within a year Donald was actually running the store, though he was then only eighteen. Donald seemed to have an instinctive knack for what he always called 'merchandising,' and by the time he was twenty-one he had developed his father's store from a musty old-fashioned pharmacy into a modern cut-rate drugstore that was slowly driving the other two pharmacies in the neighborhood out of business.

'Donald never got on too well with old Mr. Mannering, though he always liked Jonathan. So when he came of age, he somehow managed to have himself declared Douglas's guardian, evicted the tenants from his house, and moved himself and Douglas into it. That same year he bought out one of the stores whose business he had stolen, which started the Lawson chain. Ten years later the chain covered the state and twenty years later spread all over the nation.' She stopped, as though in puzzlement. 'I don't seem to be telling much about Douglas, do I?'

'No,' I said. 'But it's all background. Keep it up.'

She hesitated, collecting her thoughts. 'Donald married, and his wife bore the two children — I still seem to be on Donald, but he played such an important part in Douglas's life, there isn't much story without him. Donald rather spoiled Douglas, you see, or at least tried to. I never knew anyone as fond of a younger brother as Donald was of Douglas. He treated him like a pampered son rather than a brother. Never allowed him to work as he had, sent him through medical school and then on for graduate work in psychiatry — Douglas decided he didn't like psychiatry after wasting a year, and went into general practice, after all — set him up in practice, and in general behaved like a doting father. It's really amazing Douglas turned out as unspoiled as he did.' She paused. 'That's all there is.'

'Wait,' I said. 'You've just got Douglas out of school and in practice. Bring him up to the present.'

'There really isn't much more to tell,' she said slowly. 'I've known Douglas ten years, and he's always been charming and witty and a trifle mocking, as though everyone else was put on earth for his personal amusement, but he's not in the least snobbish. He just seems to enjoy life in a rather carefree manner, and he's inclined to be a bit of a tease. But he has a serious side, too. He's quite a good physician, for example, and has an excellent practice which he neglects only on weekends — and today, because of the funeral.

'As far as sketching his history during the ten years I've known him, absolutely nothing of any importance has happened.

He was practicing medicine when I married Donald, and he still is. He lived in the same apartment then and visited here every weekend — at least since we moved here five years ago — just as he does now. What else is there to tell?'

'This is a little personal,' I said, 'but how long have you been secretly engaged?'

'About three months.' Unaccountably she flushed deeply. 'Perhaps that seems premature with Donald dead not quite a year, but we originally planned to hold the announcement until the year was up.' For some reason she seemed to feel she had to justify herself. 'Outwardly we have obeyed all the proprieties, even tacitly agreeing not to discuss marriage plans in private until the year was up. But you can't set a timing device on your emotions as you can on your actions.'

I asked, 'How long before your actual understanding had Dr. Lawson been carrying this secret love in his heart?'

She looked at me blankly.

'I mean,' I suggested in a cautious tone, 'did his love precede your husband's death?'

She smiled. 'Douglas and I have always been fond of each other, but in an entirely different way when Donald was alive. It simply would never have occurred to Douglas to covet Donald's wife. Donald was his big brother, his father, and his boyhood hero all rolled into one. I doubt that he ever really took a good look at me until he finally began to realize Donald was gone forever and I was a widow. And that was at least six months after the accident, for he took Donald's death pretty hard.

'If you think Douglas in some miraculous manner staged the accident that killed my husband — incidentally putting himself in the hospital — then murdered Don Junior and tried to kill Grace so I'd inherit the money and he could marry me for it, I'm afraid you'd never be able to convince me. In the first place he has plenty of money of his own. I'd estimate his practice brings in at least twenty-five thousand a year, and deducting the four years he was a Medical Corps major, he's had eleven years of practice. In the second place, you yourself said he was no longer a suspect insofar as Grace is concerned, because he was the one who rescued her from the pool. In the third place, while he was never over-fond of Don Junior, Douglas wouldn't hurt Grace for all the money in the world.'

She smiled in reminiscence. 'I recall when Grace was fifteen, she got mad at Douglas about something — some boy she had been forbidden to see, I believe it was. She confided to Douglas that she was seeing him anyway, and Douglas told her father. Grace declared Douglas was a snitch, refused to speak to him for two weeks, and said she'd never speak to him again as long as she lived. Of course she got over it, but until she did Douglas was literally sick. All the humor and mockery went out of him as though cut off by a switch. He actually lost weight, and I believe he'd have ended up sick in bed if Grace hadn't decided he was punished enough and forgiven him.'

I said, 'He snitched again when she and Arnold got married.'

'Only to me,' Ann said quickly. 'And that doesn't count. Douglas knows I wouldn't hurt Grace any more than he would.'

'There's something I don't understand about you,' I said. 'Here you have a perfectly legal right to twenty million dollars, yet you withheld what you knew simply to avoid hurting Grace's feelings. I'm afraid for that amount I'd be willing to hurt nearly anyone's feelings.'

'Probably it's hard for other people to understand,' she said quietly, 'but I already have all the material comforts the Lawson millions could bring me. All the inheritance means to me is a pile of paper certificates to hold in a safe-deposit box, for I have no interest in operating the business. But the main reason is I feel I have no moral right to the money. Donald intended it to be Grace's, and I'm sure he would have approved of Arnold and given his blessing had he known him. What it boils down to is, the loss of Grace's friendship isn't worth twenty million dollars to me.'

'Think you'll lose it?' I asked.

She shook her head. 'Not now. But had I disclosed the secret rather than Arnold,

I'm afraid I would have. Grace would regard that as cheating — which, of course, it would have been.'

'Will she be mad at Arnold?'

'Probably. But since he did it through the unselfish motive of saving her life, no doubt she'll get over it.'

'Does the money mean so much to Grace?' I asked. 'The day I met her she seemed to think it unfair of her father not to have left it to you.'

'It isn't the money so much,' Ann explained. 'It's more about Grace's code of behavior. In many respects she's still a little girl. She loves an intrigue such as her secret marriage, with millions the forfeit if she was caught. Since she regards me as her family, I doubt that she really cares whose name the money is in; but if she suspected I wanted to get it away from her by trickery, she'd fight like a tiger.'

'Will you accept the inheritance now that everything is open and aboveboard?'

'I suppose I'll have to. No, that isn't being honest. I suppose if I wanted I could sign everything back to Grace. But if Donald had left everything to me in the first place, of course I would have accepted it, so there's no reason for me not to now. Of course I'll give Grace everything she wants, and I'll make her my sole heir.' She smiled slightly. 'Jonathan's going to grow tired of me changing my will.'

'Let's go on to Arnold Tate,' I said.

Arnold, it developed, had cropped up about a month after Ann became a widow. Aside from what I already knew about him, I learned he was from Kansas City, his father was a high school teacher, and he had one younger brother, who was in the Navy. Ann had never met his folks.

About the servants Ann knew practically nothing. None of the five were married, and all lived in, but aside from that she knew nothing of their various backgrounds or private lives, since Maggie did all the hiring. Maggie and Jason had been working when she married Donald Lawson. When they moved to the present house five years before, Edmund, a maid and a helper for Jason had been added. The latter two positions had had several turnovers, and Kate and Karl had both been working only about six months. Karl, she believed, had graduated from high school in an orphanage just before coming to work here. Kate had been a maid somewhere else, but Ann did not know where.

Deciding I had gleaned all the information I could from her, I closed the interview by suggesting we go up to check on the conditions of Grace and Fausta. She rose with an air of relief and preceded me up the stairs.

Grace Lawson's room was the third to the right from the stair head. The door just before it stood open, and as Ann reached it she stopped without warning. Not many people know I have a false leg, and sometimes I almost forget it myself. But at this moment I was reminded of it suddenly, for when Ann stopped, my good leg was swinging forward and my entire weight rested on an aluminum foot. With a false leg, once you start to take a step, you can't stop. I finished the step and crashed 190 pounds into Ann's soft body.

As she stumbled away from me, I grabbed her to keep her from falling, and she clawed at my shoulders in an endeavor to prevent the same thing. After a couple of erratic waltz steps, we ended in the middle of the hall with my hands locked behind her back and her arms circling my neck. For a surprised moment we remained in that position, staring at each other.

'Don't let me interrupt,' said a cold voice.

Without uncoupling, both of us glanced at Dr. Lawson, who frowned at us from the door of the room in front of which Ann had started to halt. At the same moment Fausta appeared in the doorway of Grace's bedroom. Her eyes drooped half-shut and she weaved drunkenly, regaining her balance by planting a hand on either side of the doorway.

'Manny Moon,' she said in a dull, hangover-laden voice, 'you turn loose that Jezebel.'

17

By dinnertime Grace was also awake and up, though neither she nor Fausta were in any mood for dinner. Neither had any idea of what had happened to her, remembering nothing after finishing her drink at the pool.

By the time Grace awakened, Dr. Lawson had recovered from his peeve at finding his fiancée in my arms, and tended to consider the incident rather funny. Fausta, however, continued to regard her hostess with belligerent suspicion and to maintain a cold hauteur toward me.

After dinner another group conclave was held, during which it was again decided Grace should leave the house. Grace, subdued by her experience in the pool, sick to her stomach and with a throbbing headache, offered no resistance to anything.

'Since you all know Grace was at El

Patio before,' I told the group, 'there isn't much point in trying to conceal she's going back there. I'm inclined to agree with Arnold Tate that since his announcement of the secret marriage, there will be no further attempts on Grace's life. But I have no intention to take any chances. For the benefit of whichever one of you it applies to, there is only one stairway to the upper floor at El Patio. Mr. Greene here will be at the top of it all night with a cocked pistol, so if you have any urgent reason to talk to Grace, phone her. There's a phone in the apartment listed under Miss Moreni's name.'

Leaving them with this cheerful information, we returned to El Patio in Moldy Greene's convertible. We arrived about eight o'clock, the hour Fausta usually began floating from table to table greeting customers. But tonight she was in no condition to play the charming hostess. She and Grace retired together, locking the apartment door from inside.

I helped Moldy set up a folding cot across the doorway to Fausta's apartment, watched while he made it up and tucked his automatic under the pillow, and gave him some final instructions before leaving him.

'I'll be back at eight in the morning,' I told him. 'Until then Grace stays in that apartment even if you have to tie her. Don't let anyone in, and don't let her out for any reason.'

'Suppose we have a fire?'

I contemplated him moodily. 'Just puncture your head and let the water spurt on the flames.'

At the bar downstairs I found Vance Logan listed at apartment 217 of the Grand Towers. The address struck me as rather peculiar for an ex-chauffeur, since the Grand Towers is an apartment hotel catering almost exclusively to the wealthy. The directory indicated he had a single-party phone, but since I preferred to walk in on him unannounced before he had time to mull over what I might want with him, I skipped phoning in advance.

A taxi took me to the Grand Towers. I had the driver park in the nearest vacancy to the entrance, and told him to wait.

The Towers is one of those residential

hotels with a small but expensively furnished lobby and a call desk behind which
no one ever seems to be on duty. A buzzer
with a mother-of-pearl button was mounted
at one end of the desk, presumably for the
summoning of the manager in case you
happened to want to rent a three-hundred-
dollar-a-month apartment.

I walked past the buzzer, past a
self-service elevator, and climbed the
stairs to the second floor. Here I found
a long hallway of oak paneling, floored
with a gray carpet about as thick as the
mattress on my bed. I waded through
the nap of the carpet to a door marked
217. I had my choice of a bronze door
knocker in the shape of a lion's head, or
another mother-of-pearl button. I tried
the button first, and thought I heard faint
chimes, but could not be sure. When
nothing happened after nearly a minute, I
reached for the knocker.

As I thrust my fingers against the lion's
nose, his head moved away from me
slightly. I glanced sidewise and saw my
movement had pushed the door open a
crack. I tried the button again and this

time heard the chimes distinctly.

When no one answered, I pushed the door open the rest of the way and looked in. It was not yet quite dark but heavy draperies were pulled across the three windows opposite me. Two floor lamps were on in the front room, and by their light I could see the apartment was furnished in accordance with the high rent charged.

It was also furnished with a corpse.

He wore a blue dressing gown and he sat in a deep armchair facing the door. An untouched highball in which the ice had long ago melted stood on an end table next to his chair. I judged him to have been in his early thirties, and he would not have been bad-looking if there had been a top to his head.

Closing the door with my elbow, I made a tour of the whole apartment without touching anything. It contained a bedroom, bath, kitchenette, and dinette in addition to the front room, and no murderers were hiding in any of them. Back in the front room I stooped to examine the gun clutched in the dead man's right hand. It was a P-38.

Grasping his dressing gown sleeve, I gently pulled his arm away from the side of the chair until the light fell on the gun's serial number. I recognized the number because it was my P-38.

Using my handkerchief, I used the apartment's phone to call Warren Day's apartment.

'Listen, Moon,' he greeted me, 'I got office hours, and nine at night isn't one of them. Whose body you got this time?'

'I'm not sure,' I said. 'But I think his name is Vance Logan.'

'Judas Priest!' he exploded. 'Why don't you stay home nights?'

'I'm at apartment two-seventeen of the Grand Towers,' I told him. 'The apartment is listed under Vance Logan, who was chauffeuring Donald Lawson Senior about a year ago when Lawson was killed in an auto accident. If this guy is Vance Logan, he is supposed to have committed suicide because he's got a gun in his hand. The only catch is, the gun belongs to me, and is the one I reported heisted by Harry the Horse and Dude Garrity.'

'I'll be right over,' he said wearily. 'Don't touch anything.'

The police arrived with sirens wide open and a callous disregard for the nervous system of the fat hotel manager, who popped out of the wall someplace the minute Warren Day walked into the room. The manager seemed to think the murder was a deliberate plot by the police to destroy his hotel's reputation, and I got the impression his solution to the killing would have been to drop the body in the river and forget the whole thing.

'I knew I should have asked that man for references!' he wailed when he saw the corpse.

'Shut up and get out of the way!' Day snarled at him.

The next half-hour was a madhouse of popping flash bulbs, fingerprint dust, and barked orders from the inspector. A medical examiner fixed the time of death as somewhere between twelve and twenty-four hours earlier, and the hotel manager identified the body as that of Vance Logan. Vance departed in a wicker basket just as the first reporters arrived.

The inspector gathered the reporters around him in the hall and said, 'The victim is Vance Logan and this is his apartment. He was found by Manville Moon, who was visiting him on business. He had a German automatic in his hand and a bullet in his head. Been dead several hours when discovered. On the surface it looks like suicide, but we think it's murder and have already dug up several important clues. We have a lead on the suspected killer — or killers — and expect to make an arrest within twenty-four hours. No stone will be left unturned to — '

'Who's the suspected killer?' a reporter from the *Post* asked. 'Off the record, of course.'

The inspector glared at him. 'No stone will be left unturned to bring the murderer to justice speedily. You may quote me as saying outrages such as this will not be tolerated as long as I remain chief of Homicide, and my department will not rest until the culprit is safely behind bars.' He paused, peered around the circle of bored faces, and snapped,

'No further statement.'

'Who was this guy, Inspector?' asked the reporter from the *Post*. 'Give with a little background.'

'Get it from the hotel manager, here,' Day said, jerking his thumb at the fat man.

Then he took my arm and led me back into the apartment. Before he closed the door, we could hear the manager saying appealingly, 'Couldn't you fellows say 'a downtown hotel' instead of Grand' Towers'? Mr. Logan wasn't one of the regular residents, you see. Only been here a few months, and — '

The inspector shut the door and cut off the rest of it. Lieutenant Hannegan idly rested on the front room sofa, but the rest of the police horde had departed.

'All right, Moon,' Day said wearily, 'now give with the dope.'

Briefly I explained how and why I happened to find the body.

'On the surface it looks like this ties Donald Senior's death in with Don Junior's and the attempts on young Grace,' the inspector said, scratching his bald head. 'If you hadn't already connected this Logan with the Lawson case, it might have passed as a suicide. But why you suppose those two mugs were stupid enough to use a gun that could be traced?'

I shrugged. 'It's a war souvenir. Must be thousands of unregistered German P-38s floating around. Maybe they thought my mind worked like theirs and I wouldn't have registered it.'

'Is it registered?'

I looked at him coldly. 'If you think back, Inspector, you've had me in jail three times on charges you dreamed up but couldn't make stick. Every time you took my gun away and checked the registration.'

The three occasions were sore spots for both of us. Day shifted the conversation to a new channel. 'If we could nail those two mugs, we'd be a long way toward clearing this whole thing up. I can't understand where they've holed up, because every man on the force has their photographs and has memorized their descriptions.' He peered at me over his glasses. 'You got any more bright ideas?'

'One,' I said. 'How about giving me authority to retrace everything you did in such a hurry Saturday night and Sunday morning? Talk to whoever performed the autopsy on Don, for example, and to the handwriting expert who examined the so-called suicide note.'

'Don't you think we know how to compile evidence?' Day growled. 'Think we need an ex-stevedore to check on us?'

I shrugged.

Glumly, he examined my face. 'Tell you what,' he said finally. 'I been thinking of assigning someone to go back over that ground, anyway. It will save a man if you do it instead. But I want your guarantee you'll report everything you find out.'

'Why should I hold out on you?' I asked irritably. 'I'm as eager to catch this killer as you are.'

'Then be at headquarters at nine in the morning. After we get your statement about tonight on paper, I'll give you a note to Doc Halloran and Professor Quisby, so you can check back on the autopsy and suicide note.'

'Fine. Need me for anything else now?'

'Not till nine in the morning. Be there on time.'

My taxi was still waiting and the bill had mounted accordingly. 'If you do this often, you could afford to buy a car,' the driver told me.

'I have one,' I said. 'It's in the garage having a fireplug pried loose from its radiator.'

He shook his head sympathetically. 'These new cars can't take the same knocking around they did ten years ago.'

I told him to take me home.

18

At eight the next morning I found Moldy sitting on his cot in his undershirt and pants, in which apparently he had slept. He told me someone was up in the apartment because he had heard movements, but neither Grace nor Fausta had yet appeared.

Leaning across the cot, I knocked on the door and almost immediately it was opened by Fausta. She wore a dirndl and a white silk peasant blouse that exposed shoulders the color of coffee with cream, and just as appetizing to a man who had not yet had breakfast. Her tangy perfume mixed with the aroma of frying eggs in the background.

'Gee, that smells good!' I remarked, climbing over Moldy's bed.

'It is called Nocturnal Menace,' Fausta said, tipping an ear for me to sniff.

'I meant the eggs,' I said absently, walking on by her toward the kitchen.

I had taken two steps when her spike heel caught me in the seat of the pants. I spun around to find her standing with hands balled against her hips and a dangerous glint in her eyes.

'The perfume is nice, too,' I said, backing into the kitchen.

Grace Lawson, minus her Mickey Finn hangover and looking like a twelve-year-old kid in a blue playsuit that exhibited six inches of tanned stomach and all of her slim legs, was setting the table. 'We've been expecting you, Mr. Moon,' she said. 'Is Mr. Greene up yet?'

'Just barely,' I said, staring at the brief shorts and briefer jacket. 'Look, I'm not letting you out of my sight today, but I've got a lot of running around to do and I'll have to take you along. You're not planning to wear that outfit on the street, are you?'

'Certainly,' she said in an offended tone. 'All the girls dress like this in this weather.'

'Not when they're with me,' I said definitely, 'unless I'm going to the beach. You get on a dress.'

'Hah!' Fausta put in. 'If her stepmother dressed like that, you would goggle with the eyes and say nothing. Let the child alone.'

Moldy came in to join us for breakfast, having donned a shirt and his shoes. He had not yet shaved, but with his face it made little difference.

I decided to let Grace's costume ride until after breakfast, which was a mistake, for when I brought it up again, Fausta turned obstinate and declared she was going along with us in a similar costume. Flouncing into the bedroom, she returned wearing a yellow bandana in place of the peasant blouse and yellow silk shorts in place of the dirndl. 'Ye Gods!' I said. 'You look like you're in your underwear!'

'I think she looks good,' Moldy contributed in an admiring tone.

I glanced at my watch, saw it was twenty of nine, and gave up the argument.

'You get stuck with the dishes, chum,' I told Moldy.

Since El Patio did not open till noon, the bar was deserted. I used the bar phone to call the nearest cab stand, and ten minutes later we were on our way to police headquarters. It was exactly nine when I told Danny Blake, the desk sergeant, to inform Day I was there. Danny buzzed the inspector's office without taking his eyes from Fausta's bare stomach.

'You stay here,' I instructed the two girls. 'The sergeant hasn't completed his inspection yet.'

A uniformed stenographer with an open notebook on his knee sat in one corner of Warren Day's office. Day was seated at his desk. I sat down on a vacant chair.

'All right, Moon,' he said sourly, 'give your story over again for the record.'

Slowly, so as not to get ahead of the stenographer's racing pencil, I went over the events leading to my discovery of Vance Logan's body. I started with my conversation with Ann Lawson, at which I first learned of the chauffeur's existence; then explained that the possibility of Donald Lawson Senior's death having been murder instead of an accident had occurred to me, and this was the reason I had wanted to interview Logan. When I finished, the inspector nodded without asking further questions, and the stenographer left the room.

'Don't suppose there's any chance of getting my gun back for a while, is there?' I asked.

'No, not till it's been presented as evidence at a trial.'

'That means about a year after the guys are caught,' I said glumly. 'Get a report on that doped Coke yet?'

'Yeah. Chloral hydrate. Exactly 1.5 grams to the bottle, which the lab says is a pretty heavy dose, but safely under a fatal one.'

I said, 'How about your check on the finances of our suspects?'

'Judas Priest!' he said. 'I just put a guy on it this morning.'

'Think you'll have it by tomorrow?'

'I'd better,' he said grimly, 'or a certain young college cop is going to get bounced right back in the commissioner's lap for assignment to another department.'

'While you're at it,' I suggested, 'why

don't you add Vance Logan to the list?'

'What for?'

'Didn't it strike you a little strange that an ex-chauffeur lived at the Grand Towers?'

'I guess that is a pretty fancy place.' Fishing a blank scrap of paper from the litter on his desk, the inspector made a penciled note.

I asked, 'How about that note of introduction you were going to give me?'

Pawing through the litter again, he found a piece of memo paper and tossed it to me. It was addressed both to Dr. Thomas Halloran of City Hospital and Professor Laurence Quisby of the State Teachers' College. It stated that I was investigating the death of Donald Lawson Jr. in a semi-official capacity, and asked that I be given co-operation.

'The first is the guy who performed the autopsy,' Day said. 'He's a second-year intern at City Hospital.'

'I know him,' I said.

'The second is the guy we use as our handwriting expert. Teaches educational psychology, whatever that is. Handwriting is his hobby.'

'Any chance of taking along Don's suicide note?' I asked.

The inspector frowned at me.

'I won't lose it. But there isn't much point in talking to Professor Quisby unless I have the note for him to examine again.'

'Humph,' he said. Leaning over, he jerked open a desk drawer and removed a cardboard file folder. He opened it, removed a sheet of paper, and tossed it to me. 'Lose that and I'll slap a warrant on you for destroying evidence.'

I folded the note into my breast pocket. Another twenty minutes passed before the police stenographer returned with my statement typed up in triplicate. By the time I had read it over and signed it, it was after ten o'clock.

The city morgue is in the basement of the City Hospital, and that is where I found young Dr. Halloran. I left Fausta and Grace in the anteroom, which had posted about its walls a series of particularly revolting pictures of bodies in various stages of decomposition, and followed a lank, dour-faced morgue attendant back

247

to the laboratory.

Dr. Tom Halloran was a thin, youngish man with slightly stooped shoulders, an eager expression, and ears that flared outward like twin air scoops. His stoop came from a habit of thrusting his head forward inquisitively, and this, combined with his eager expression and cocked ears, created the unnerving impression that he was constantly waiting with bated breath for you to say something. I had had dealings with him before, and though we were not particularly good friends, we were on a first-name basis. It was not the young doctor's fault we weren't better friends, for he practically folded me to his bosom whenever we met. But invariably our conversation turned to the morbid subject of overripe cadavers.

'Manny Moon!' he said heartily, looking up from a microscope under which he undoubtedly had something gruesome. He advanced across the small room with an outstretched hand.

I shook it without enthusiasm and showed him the note from Warren Day.

'Donald Lawson,' he said. 'I ought to

remember him. Homicide dragged me down here at one a.m. to perform the autopsy. A real stinker, he was. Been in the sun nearly a week, and all mashed up on top of it. Seven feet of entrails I had laid out on the drain-board before I was through.'

'What I wanted was your findings,' I said. 'In non-technical terms, if you don't mind.'

'Sure,' he said, rubbing his hands together. 'I can tell you from memory, without even going to the card index. Plain case of gravity. Hardly an unbroken bone in his body.'

I said, 'We're pretty sure it wasn't an accident, but there's still some question if it was suicide or murder. How complete an autopsy did you make?'

'The works. That's what Homicide asked for, and that's what they got. Of course I can't tell you how he came to fall, but nothing but the fall killed him.'

'I wondered if possibly he might have been unconscious when he fell.'

Halloran shrugged. 'No way to tell that. He might even have been dead. I mean, if someone bashed his head in with a hammer, then tossed him off of whatever it was he fell from, we'd have no way of sorting the hammer blow out from all the other concussions.'

I said, 'I meant was he drunk or doped or anything like that? We've had another instance of chloral hydrate being used in this same case.'

The young doctor shook his head. 'Not a chance. We tested for everything. Found a slight accumulation of alcohol in the brain, but not enough to make him unconscious. More like he'd had a few beers.'

'That's all I wanted to know,' I told him. 'Thanks for the information.'

'Glad to help,' he said. 'But take a look at this before you leave, anyway. You'll get a kick out of it.' Opening the drawer behind him, he drew out a small, dark-colored object resembling a dried fig. He laid it on my palm.

'What is it?' I inquired.

'A hobo's ear. Guy was in a knife fight, and this came in two days after he was buried in Potter's Field. A street sweeper found it.' He stooped to pick the object from the floor, where it had fallen from my palm.

'Sorry,' I muttered. 'Clumsy of me.'

Before he could find more curiosities to interest me, I made my way back to where Fausta and Grace were waiting. The two women were staring fascinatedly at a photograph of a marble slab on which lay a torso without arms, legs, or head. The lanky morgue attendant was staring just as fascinatedly at the legs of his beautiful visitors.

'If you can tear yourselves away from that art, I'll buy you both a drink,' I said. 'I'm having a double myself.'

19

City ordinance forbids the establishment of a tavern within two hundred yards of a hospital, which meant a two-block walk before we could get a drink. We barely made it, and while Fausta sipped a rum Coke and Grace a plain Coke, I anchored my breakfast down with a double rye.

Professor Laurence Quisby was teaching a class when we arrived at the State Teachers' College, a group of three buildings in the center of the business district. There was little college atmosphere about the school. There was no campus. The buildings came right to the edge of the sidewalk, just as did the other office buildings in the area.

A clerk in the administration building told us Professor Quisby would be free at noon, and since it was already past eleven-thirty, I told him we would wait. He showed us to a small office which had Professor Quisby's name inscribed on the door and offered us the comfort of three straight-backed chairs.

The professor turned out to be a round, gray-haired man with a sad face and a Van Dyke beard. He glanced at Fausta and Grace without surprise and without the faintest flicker of admiration in his eyes, which led me to believe he was not long for this world. He lowered himself into the chair behind his desk, turned sad eyes on me, and waited without speaking.

I pushed Warren Day's note under his nose without speaking, either. He read it, pushed it back, and elevated one eyebrow.

'This is Miss Grace Lawson, Professor,' I said, indicating the girl. 'She's the sister of the lad who wrote that note. And this is Miss Fausta Moreni, who has no connection with the case, but just came along for the ride.' He offered a slight nod to each. 'We've come pretty close to a dead end on this thing,' I told him. 'So we're rechecking all the original evidence.' Removing the suicide note from my inner pocket, I pushed it across to him. 'I understand you positively identified the handwriting here as the deceased's by comparing it with other handwriting of his.'

With his eyes fixed on the note, he nodded a depressed affirmative.

'I also understand you said the writing indicated emotional strain.'

He gave the same signal.

'Can you tell me anything else at all about the note?' I persisted.

When he finally spoke his voice was surprisingly deep and resonant. 'The paper was eight and a half inches wide and seven and one-eighth inches long, indicating it was part of a piece of standard typing paper, either the ten-and-a-half-inch or thirteen-and-a-half-inch length. Probably the former, since two samples on ten-and-a-half-inch paper with the same watermark were included in the material furnished me for comparison. A shred of gummed fabric clung to the upper edge, indicating the sheet had been ripped from a pad of typing paper, possibly the same pad from which the other two specimens came. The bottom had been cut off with a pair of scissors.'

He lifted sorrowful eyes from the note

to my face. 'I mention these details because I've been thinking about this note ever since I made my report. For some reason the police insisted on an examination in the middle of the night, and while I made a thorough comparison, the odd length of the paper did not strike me as peculiar until afterward. I've been meaning to contact the police, but you've saved me the trouble.'

'How do you mean, odd length?' I asked.

'Seven and one-eighth inches.' Then he asked in the same patient but hopeless tone he probably employed when prompting students during recitation, 'What length would half a sheet be?'

I did some mental arithmetic and asked, 'You mean twice seven and one-eighth inches would be fourteen and a quarter, and there is no such standard-length paper?'

His expression bespoke the frustrated educator, weighted down by the stupidity of humanity, who finally has succeeded in inciting an intelligent answer from one of his students. He almost smiled when he nodded.

'And ordinarily,' I continued to guess, 'if a person wanted less than a full sheet of paper, he would simply fold it and tear it in half, not measure off an odd length and cut it with a pair of scissors?'

This time his nod was accompanied by a definite smile.

Retrieving the suicide note, I examined it myself, noting that though the writing wavered, the lines moved geometrically across the page and were spaced nearly a half inch apart. The last line was only about a quarter inch from the bottom. I tossed the paper back to the professor and imitated him by raising one eyebrow.

'I don't need to examine it again,' he said ponderously. 'I had it under a microscope for twenty minutes.' He traced the bottom line with his finger. 'This last line — 'Explain things to Grace, Uncle Doug' — originally, there was a period between 'Grace' and 'Uncle Doug,' then a tail was added to make it a comma. At the time I assumed the writer had simply made a mistake, then gone back and corrected it, for the ink and pen used were the same, and there seemed to be no difference in its age. Of course, with only a single comma for a specimen, it's impossible to say whether the same writer made the correction.'

I said slowly, 'Then this could be part of a longer note, with the bottom cut off and its meaning changed by the addition of a comma?' He treated me to another nod. 'Originally the word 'Grace' may have ended a sentence,' I went on, 'which would make 'Uncle Doug' the first two words of another sentence that continued on another line.' Now I had him nodding almost with enthusiasm. 'But there's no way to guess what the rest of the message may have been,' I ended lamely.

Surprisingly, he smiled. 'If you can bring me the pad on which this was written, I might be able to restore the full text.'

I looked at him blankly.

'Indentations,' he said simply.

I saw the idea. The pressure of the pen would imprint an invisible record on the second sheet of the pad, a record which could be made visible in the laboratory.

Suddenly Grace spoke. 'I know the pad

you're talking about. I've seen it on Don's desk. He kept it in the upper right-hand drawer.'

'Then that's our next stop,' I said, rising. 'Thanks a lot, Professor. If we're lucky, we'll bring the pad back this afternoon.' He gave us a final nod as we departed.

We caught a cruising cab at the next corner and arrived at Willow Dale twenty minutes later. As I was telling the taxi driver to wait, Grace and Fausta hurried on to the side door. By the time I reached it, they had disappeared into the house.

When I entered the side hall, Maggie was standing with her back to me, gazing in the direction of the stairway. As I brushed past her, she looked at me disapprovingly, her catfish mouth pressed into a straight line.

The desk in Don's room was a flattop with an upright back full of alcoves. Fausta was pulling everything out of the alcoves, while Grace went through the drawers. Being the executive type, I sat on the edge of the bed and watched.

Both girls finished at once and stopped

258

to look at each other.

'It's gone!' Grace announced.

I rose from the bed. 'Now if you amateurs will get out of the way, I'll show you a professional search.'

I went over every inch of the desk, including pulling out each drawer and looking behind it. Then I tackled the dresser, the closet, and every other place of possible concealment in the room.

When I finally gave up, Grace said, 'That's what I said. It's gone.'

Ann Lawson stuck her head in the door. Before she could ask any questions, I said, 'We're looking for a pad of typing paper that used to belong to Don. Any idea who could have taken it from his desk?'

'No,' she said, staring at us all as though suspicious of our sanity. 'Is it important?'

'Yes, but apparently someone else realized its importance before we did.' I turned to Fausta and Grace. 'We may as well get back to town. I have some more calls to make.'

Grace said, 'It's getting on toward one.

Let's have some lunch first.'

'Yes,' Ann invited. 'If you don't stay, I'll have to lunch alone.'

There were only four of us at lunch, all of the weekend guests having finally returned to their respective homes. I was in a depressed mood at having missed the only tangible clue yet appearing, and this probably threw a pall over the others' spirits, for it was a silent meal. We returned to town immediately afterward.

At the city hall I dismissed the cab and led Fausta and Grace to the city clerk's office. The girls' hot-weather costumes attracted attention here, too, although this time it was disapproval rather than admiration. The clerk who waited on us was a woman. She was a plump girl in her mid-twenties, red-faced from the stifling heat. Her examination of my two companions' cool outfits was a mixture of disdain and envy.

I told her I would like a copy of the death record of Donald Lawson Sr., who had died the previous August 27th. We waited outside the cage while she thumbed through a huge book in one corner, then disappeared into another room. After a few moments we heard the clatter of a typewriter. Ten minutes later she thrust a notarized sheet of paper under the wicket and said, 'Fifty cents, please.' I gave her a half dollar.

The top half of the death certificate listed all of the vital statistics such as name, date and place of birth, sex, color, etc., and the bottom half contained the details of death. According to it Lawson had been dead on arrival at Millard Hospital, the cause of death being suffocation due to a crushed upper vertebra closing the larynx. I deduced this to mean he died of a broken neck. No other injuries were recorded, and no autopsy had been performed. A Dr. Milton Standish had signed the certificate.

I had a sudden idea. 'What was the date your brother ran off and got married?' I asked Grace.

'Why — let's see, it was three years ago in the fall. October, I think.'

'Were they married in town?'

'Across the river somewhere. By a

justice of the peace.'

'Maybe they got the license here,' I said. I called the red-faced girl over again. 'See if you can find a marriage license application for Donald Lawson Junior. About October three years ago.'

She returned to the corner and began turning the pages of a second large volume. Reaching the proper page, her finger traveled down it to the center and stopped. 'Want a certified copy?' she asked.

'Just the information.'

Her eyes returned to the book. 'October second. Donald Martin Lawson Junior, age twenty-one, and Mary Katherine Malone, age eighteen.'

'He lied about his age,' Grace said. 'He was only eighteen.'

'Mary Katherine Malone,' I said, frowning. 'Ever hear of her, Grace?'

She shook her head. 'I do remember now that her name was Mary. But none of us except Don and Daddy ever saw her. And after Daddy had the marriage annulled, it was as much as your life was worth to even mention it around the house.'

As we went down the city hall steps, I

was still puzzling over a vague familiarity about the girl's name.

'Mary Katherine Malone,' I repeated aloud, and then it hit me. 'Kate Malone!' I said to Grace. 'For a moment the 'Mary Katherine' threw me.'

Grace stared at me with her mouth open. 'You can't possibly mean our maid is my sister-in-law!'

20

For the second time that day I took a taxi to Willow Dale, but this time I went alone, for I wanted to speak to Kate privately, and I had no intention of letting Grace out of my sight anywhere in the vicinity of her home. First we returned to El Patio, where I remanded my charge to Moldy Greene's custody.

'Don't move two feet from her side until I get back,' I told him.

He nodded his flat head. 'Sure. Suppose she wants to go to the powder room?'

'Then ask Fausta for instructions,' I said patiently.

At the Lawson home I found Ann sitting on the veranda sipping an iced lemonade.

'May I talk to Kate somewhere privately?' I asked her.

'Certainly,' she said, rising and preceding me into the house. 'Go back to the den and I'll send her in.' She showed no surprise at the request, apparently having become adjusted to the idea that I was going to pop in and out at odd moments on strange missions while the investigation was going on.

When Kate showed up in the den a few minutes later, I asked her to sit down, then took a seat behind the desk myself. Without preamble I asked, 'Why did you conceal you were the girl who eloped with Don Lawson three years ago?'

She turned dead white, leaned back in her chair, and passed out cold.

Fortunately I had a little experience with fainting women, once having had a female client who fainted at regular intervals. I employed the same treatment my fainting client had me use. Grasping the girl's shoulders, I bent her forward until her head hung down between her knees. In a few moments she snorted twice, wagged her head back and forth, then weakly sat up.

'Want me to get you a glass of water?' I asked.

She shook her head, closed her eyes,

and leaned back. I waited until her color had returned.

'Let's start over,' I suggested. 'Why did you conceal you were Don Lawson's ex-wife?'

'I'll get out of town tonight,' she said in a weak, pleading voice. 'Please, mister. Give me a break.'

'Why should you leave town?'

She straightened, and a cautious expression replaced the fright in her face. 'You mean you aren't going to — ' She broke off and asked crisply, 'What was it you wanted, Mr. Moon?'

I said gently, 'Let's get something straight, Kate. I'm interested only in whoever is trying to bump off the Lawson family. I'm not a cop, and if whatever you're afraid of doesn't concern Don's death or the attempts on Grace, I wouldn't repeat it to a soul.'

'I'm afraid I don't know what you're talking about,' she said haughtily. She rose, as if to leave the room.

'Yes you do. For some reason you thought you were in for lots of trouble if anyone discovered you were the girl who eloped with Don. That's why you kept it a secret. Apparently you thought I had come to arrest you or something. Well, I didn't. But I want to know what you're afraid of.'

'You're mistaken. I'm not afraid of anything.'

'The alternative,' I said, 'is to explain to the police. Take your choice.'

Her lips began to tremble. 'Why can't you let me alone?'

'Look, Kate,' I said reasonably, 'if you aren't tied up in this affair concerning Don and Grace, I don't care what you did that makes you afraid. Tell me and it stops right there.'

'I didn't do anything.' A tear slid down one cheek. 'The shoplifting charge was a frame-up.'

'What shoplifting charge?'

Now the tears were falling freely, and along with them the story spilled out in a supplicating tone, her eyes begging for belief. 'It was right after I married Don. When we phoned his father, he came right down to the hotel. We had registered at the Jefferson, you see. We'd both been kind of scared of what Don's father would say, but figured he had to know it sometime, and once we were married there wouldn't be anything he could do.'

She dabbed her tears with a handkerchief. 'That's where we were wrong. He jerked Don out of the room just like he was a kid, and left me there waiting with my mouth open. There wasn't a thing I could think of to do, so I finally just went to bed and cried all night.'

'And then?' I prodded.

'Mr. Lawson came back in the morning with three men. One was a policeman in plain clothes — he showed me his badge. The other two were the manager and the store detective of Mercer's Department Store. The store detective said, 'That's the woman,' and pointed at me, and the manager nodded his head and said, 'Yes. She's the one, all right.' Then the cop said, 'Come along, sister. You're under arrest.' I said I didn't know what they were talking about. Then Mr. Lawson explained that the store manager and the detective claimed they had caught me shoplifting at Mercer's, and wanted to swear out a warrant. He said their testimony could get me ten years in jail, but he was interceding because he wanted to avoid the publicity of his son's wife being in jail. He said he was having our marriage annulled on the grounds that Don was underage, and told me very frankly he intended to arrange things so there was no chance of us ever getting together again. I could take my choice of getting out of the state and staying out, or going to prison.'

'Did you swallow that hogwash?' I asked in astonishment.

'It wasn't hogwash,' she said. 'I don't know about the store detective, but the man who said he managed Mercer's really did, because I had returned a dress there once, and he was called to okay the exchange slip. The plain-clothes man was really a policeman, too. They took me down to police headquarters and entered a formal complaint and took my finger-prints. Then Mr. Lawson gave me five hundred dollars and told me to get out of the state. He said I wouldn't be hunted, but if I ever came back here, the charge would still be against me even if it was ten years later.'

I shook my head in wonderment. 'The things you can do with twenty million dollars! So when did you decide to take a chance and come back?'

'When Don found me. After his father died, he hired a private detective to trace me. I was working for some people in Chicago at the time. He said when he reached twenty-one, we could be married and he'd have enough money to quash the shoplifting charge, and he talked me into coming back. Just in case, I decided to go by my middle name instead of Mary, which was the name the charge was filed under.'

'I still don't see why you concealed your identity,' I said thoughtfully. 'Now that both the old man and Don are dead, it isn't likely the store manager and detective would press charges — *if* the thing was trumped up originally.'

'Don't you think so?' she asked hopefully, ignoring the innuendo tacked on the end of my last statement.

I smiled at her reassuringly. 'Don't

worry about it another minute. I know the police chief personally, and I'll explain the whole frame-up to him.'

'Oh, don't do that!' she said quickly. 'I'd rather you just let it drop. I mean, after all this time — '

'Look, Kate,' I said, tiring of the cat-and-mouse act, 'your story is even more moving than *East Lynne*, and if it weren't for one thing you'd have had me weeping in my beer. The one thing is that I *do* know Police Chief Chester personally. He was executive officer of my battalion during the war. And there isn't enough money in the world to make George Chester let the police department be used for a frame like that.'

The red started at her throat and crept upward until she was crimson to the hairline.

'I told you I wouldn't turn you in unless you were the particular murderer I'm looking for,' I said wearily. 'Outside of the Lawson family, I don't care who you killed or what other crimes you've committed. *But I want a straight story.*'

The tears started to flow again. 'What I

told you is straight, almost. I just changed it a little.'

I gave her a sour grin. 'Just the part about it being a frame, eh?'

She nodded. 'It happened a year before I met Don,' she said in a small voice. 'The judge gave me a year's suspended sentence and put me on parole. I broke parole and changed my name. My real name is Janet Whittier. Don's father checked police records just in the hope that he'd find something on me to use as a weapon. They had my picture on file, so he had me cold. Everything happened like I said, except it was parole violation they could have sent me up for.'

I rose and walked around the desk. 'All right, Kate. I'm going to check your record at headquarters, but I won't turn you in. One more question. Why did you tell us the other night that you hadn't definitely decided to marry Don?'

'Because I really hadn't.' She frowned to herself. 'I mean, I meant to marry him when I decided to come back, but after I got here — ' She shrugged hopelessly. 'I just decided I didn't really love him.'

Then she said candidly, 'I probably would have married him though. A few million dollars can make up for not loving a guy too much.'

As I started out the door, I turned and asked as an afterthought, 'Ever happen to notice a pad of typing paper in Don's desk?'

'Yes,' she said promptly. 'He didn't have a typewriter, but he always used that as letter paper.'

'Know what happened to it?'

'Sure. I gave it to Maggie for grocery lists.'

I had not expected her to know, and her answer caught me off center. She probably thought I had suddenly lost my mind, for I stood staring at her with a blank look on my face for nearly a minute, then spun around and ran from the room.

Maggie was peeling potatoes over the sink. She turned and frowned suspiciously when I burst into the kitchen.

'Maggie — ' I started to say, then stopped when I saw the pad lying on the table. 'Kate give you this?' I asked, picking it up. A list of groceries covered about a quarter of the top page.

'Yes, sir,' she said stiffly. 'Please be careful of it. It's my grocery list.'

'Have you torn off any pages?' I half-yelled. 'Since Kate gave you the pad, have you torn off any pages?'

She shook her head, a puzzled and alarmed look beginning to form in her eyes.

'Thanks,' I said, and started out with the pad.

'Hey! That's my grocery list!' Maggie shouted.

'You'll have to make another, Maggie,' I called back. 'This is murder evidence.'

Professor Laurence Quisby's last class had ended and he had gone home by the time I got back to the State Teachers' College. It was four p.m. before I finally tracked him down at home and delivered the pad.

'The pencil writing may obscure part of the message,' he said. 'But I'll do what I can. Phone me later in the evening, if you wish.'

I told him I so wished.

21

Tuesday is supposed to be Warren Day's afternoon off, but he was just leaving the office when I arrived at four-thirty. When he saw me, he wearily removed his hat, dropped it on a hook of the clothes tree next to the door, and returned to his desk.

'I been off duty four hours,' he remarked sourly. 'Where the devil's that note?'

Assuming he meant Don Lawson's suicide note, I tossed it across to him. He replaced it in the case file folder in his desk drawer, left the drawer open, and gazed down into it contemplatively. Finally he groped toward the back and brought out a whisky bottle three-fourths full. 'I never do this on duty,' he said, tipping the bottle and swallowing twice.

As he started to replace it without passing out any invitations, I remarked, 'Those were the years.'

'What were the years?' he asked.

This spiked my intended pun. He was supposed to ask, 'What years?' after which I would snap back, 'Thanks. I'll take bourbon.'

'Never mind,' I said. 'Get that bottle out and stop being such a tightwad. Anyone would think you bought it yourself.'

Not too ungraciously, he reproduced the bottle. 'It's a little raw,' he said. 'Better make it a small one.'

I told him I was willing to take a chance and matched his double swallow.

He nearly snatched the bottle from my hand when I lowered it. And when he replaced it, he locked the drawer and dropped the key in his pocket.

'All right, now,' he said. 'Give with what you found out today, if anything.'

'First tell me if anyone recognized those pictures of Don and Tate.'

He nodded. 'We hit the jackpot on every try. Don Lawson got off a bus at his gate at two-twenty a.m., and Tate was miles away on another bus at that time. So both Dr. Lawson and Tate are in the clear.'

I gave him a brief résumé of my activities since he had given me the introductory note that morning, mentioning first that there was nothing new insofar as the autopsy was concerned. When I got to the point about the suicide note being cut off with a pair of scissors, and Professor Quisby's attempt to reincarnate the original text, he pricked up his ears.

'Maybe we finally got a break,' he said. 'When will he know?'

'He told me to call him this evening. Did you ever get a copy of the Lawson will?'

'Yeah,' Day said glumly. 'Our legal expert went over it, but there's nothing there Mannering hadn't told us about.'

I asked, 'Did your college-boy cop dig up anything on our suspects' financial statuses yet?'

The inspector rummaged through the rat's nest he called an in-box, found a blue memo slip, and adjusted his glasses to read it. 'The servants first,' he said. 'Margaret Sullivan has a twenty-five-hundred-dollar savings account at Merchants' Trust, and about six months ago purchased nine thousand dollars in savings bonds.' He paused and looked at me expectantly.

'Margaret Sullivan,' I said. 'That's Maggie, the housekeeper, isn't it?'

Day nodded.

'She was left ten thousand by the will,' I reminded him. 'Subtract a thousand for taxes, a new house dress, and a bottle of wine to celebrate the inheritance, and it's all accounted for.'

The inspector nodded again. 'About how I figured. Jason Henry, the gardener, has a fifteen-hundred-dollar savings account in the same bank. Also a safety-deposit box.'

I raised one eyebrow. 'Which might contain his birth certificate,' I suggested, 'or might hold the Aga Khan's stolen jewels.'

'Right. But we can't peek in without a court order. On Kate Malone, the maid; Karl Thomas, the kid who discovered the body; and Edmund, the houseboy, we drew a blank. No record of savings in any bank in town, and no transactions through invest-ment houses. Edmund has a 'prompt payment' rating with the credit bureau, but the other two aren't known. That winds up the servants.'

'Nothing much there,' I said. 'How about the others?'

'With a couple of exceptions, the record reads like Dunn and Bradstreet. Gerald Cushing has about a hundred grand in liquid assets, and seems to be worth over a million altogether. That's only a guess by Mr. Harvey at the clearing house, because Cushing's holdings and investments are so complicated it would take a CPA a month to figure him out.

'Jonathan Mannering is worth about a quarter million, mostly in savings and gilt-edged securities. Seems he has the reputation of being a very cautious investor.'

I said, 'Ann implied he was a little conservative.'

'Ann?' the inspector asked, frowning.

'Mrs. Lawson.'

He glared at me, then went on. 'Doctor Douglas Lawson has a savings account at Riverside National of twenty thousand dollars, and a checking account of a few hundred at the same bank. Seems to have no other assets. That ends the rich kids and takes us to the average people.'

I elevated my eyebrows. 'How about Grace? Isn't she classed as a rich kid?'

Day frowned at the paper. 'I guess in a way. But she's underage and everything seems to be handled through the estate. All I got under her name is the statement, 'No records'.'

'All right,' I said. 'Get on to the average kids.'

'Abigail Stoltz has thirty-five hundred in savings, a five-hundred-dollar checking account and a collection of paintings that's supposed to be worth over twenty thousand. Last year her deposits in her checking account came to about forty-five hundred, which probably indicates her income from her own artwork.

'All Arnold Tate has is a checking account of seven hundred and fifty dollars. A year ago it was fifteen hundred, and there have been no deposits since.' He raised his head to look at me. 'The guy went to school and lived a whole year on seven hundred and fifty bucks.'

'Abe Lincoln did it on less,' I told him.

'Last of all is *Mrs.* Lawson.' He glared at me again when he emphasized the *Mrs.* 'She used to have a few stocks a while back, but got rid of them. Now she has a savings account of two thousand dollars at Riverside National and a checking account at the same bank with about eleven hundred in it.' He laid down the memo.

'And?'

'That's the works. Everything.'

I sat up straight. 'You mean Ann Lawson's total assets are only thirty-one hundred dollars?'

The inspector seemed surprised at my surprise. 'Sure. So what?'

'If you remember the will,' I said, 'Mrs. Lawson was left income from a half-million-dollar trust fund.' I did some mental computing. 'Even at three percent interest, the income would be fifteen thousand a year, and if Mannering hasn't been able to find at least three percent on a half-million-dollar investment, I wouldn't want him investing my money.'

Day still looked puzzled. 'Well?' he inquired.

'There was another interesting little item in the will.' I started ticking off on my fingers. 'The house, maintenance, servants' salaries, all were taken care of by another trust fund. Mrs. Lawson doesn't have any living expenses. So why does she have only thirty-one hundred dollars?'

Day scratched the fuzz over one ear. 'I'll bite. Why does she?'

I leaned back in my chair again. 'I've got a fair idea, but I want to sit on it awhile. Did your college boy get around to checking on the Lawsons' ex-chauffeur?'

'Vance Logan? Yeah. But it doesn't make sense.' He pushed the papers in his in box around some more until he found another blue memo slip. 'Logan had a checking account of two thousand dollars at First National. He opened it with ten thousand six months ago, ran it down to an overdraft before the end of the month, deposited five thousand more, ran through that, and has been making regular monthly deposits up to ten thousand ever since. Total deposits, including the first, came to seventy thousand dollars. First National has one of those check photostat machines that records every check clearing their bank. Most of his were cashed at North Shore Club and other gambling dives. Seems the roulette tables got most of it.'

I asked, 'Why do you say it doesn't make sense?'

Day stared at me. 'Does it make sense to you for an ex-chauffeur suddenly to start living like a millionaire?'

I nodded. 'It's the first thing in this case that does make sense. Usually you're quicker on the uptake. Logan was blackmailing someone.'

The inspector slowly straightened in his chair. 'Either I'm getting old, or this case has me going in circles,' he said disgustedly. 'A rookie could see that, but I have to have it explained by a punch-drunk ex-stevedore.'

'And you can bet your pivot tooth that's what got him killed,' I went on. 'I'm beginning to get a glimmer of light. What were the stocks you mentioned Mrs. Lawson disposed of?'

Warren Day looked at me strangely.

'What you getting at?'

'A brand new theory. What were the stocks?'

Slowly he fished the original memo back out of the in box and studied it. 'About a year ago — I haven't got the exact date — she invested a hundred thousand dollars in Marsh Chemicals. The stock immediately rose and she sold a week later at a ten percent profit. There's no record of any other market transactions either before or since.'

'So she closed out with a hundred and ten thousand?' I asked softly. 'Where is it?'

'Damn you, Moon!' the inspector said.

I looked at him in surprise. 'Don't blame me for your own evil thoughts,' I said. 'It's not my fault your criminal investigator mind puts two and two together and makes your ladylove look like a four.'

'She's not my ladylove!' Day yelled.

'I know it, Inspector,' I said soothingly. 'You're immune to love. In fact I can think of three reasons you're immune.'

'Yeah?' he said suspiciously.

'You're too sensible, too level-headed — and too old.'

'You should be in vaudeville,' he said sourly. 'You slay me.'

'If it'll make you feel better,' I said, 'there's one part of the puzzle I can't fit to Ann Lawson.'

'You don't have to make me feel better!' he yelled at me. 'Mrs. Lawson's nothing to me but another suspect!'

'I believe you,' I said. 'But here's how things stack up.' One by one I checked off items on my fingers. 'One. She has the best motive of all eleven suspects. Two. Just offhand it looks like Logan's blackmail money came from her — if it was blackmail. Maybe it was just Logan's pay for bumping the old man off. That's a possibility, but the best bet is the car was sabotaged in the same way Grace's convertible was, and Logan somehow found out who did it. Three. She hasn't an alibi either for the time of Don's death, or for any of the attacks on Grace.'

I stopped to examine the inspector's attentive but glum face. 'The part of the puzzle I can't fit to Ann,' I said, 'is the two gunmen. It's the thing that's puzzled me most about the case from the beginning. How did she contact them?'

Warren Day merely peered over his glasses at me, waiting.

'How would any of the people in this case contact them, for that matter?' I went on. 'They're all reputable people, at least on the surface. The average person would have no more idea of how to go about meeting a couple of underworld killers than I would have about getting an introduction to Josef Stalin.'

'That's a minor point we can clear up when we take Garrity and Harry the Horse,' the inspector said. His expression disapproved of me heartily, but his tone was one of begrudging agreement. 'I think your reasoning points in the right direction. But we haven't a nickel's worth of proof. We can't very well pull in anyone as influential as Mrs. Lawson and sweat out a confession on the basis of a theory. We'd have a hundred lawyers on our backs in a minute.'

I nodded agreement. 'Unless the suicide note Quisby's working on tells us something, you've only got one chance. Take Garrity and Sommerfield alive and beat the name of their employer out of them. Incidentally, you got a file on a parole violator named Janet Whittier?'

'Who's she? How's she fit in?'

I told him I didn't know whether she fitted in at all, but if she did I'd tell him about it after we looked up the record. After some grumbling, he took me back to the record room and we looked up the file.

The picture accompanying the record was that of a seventeen-year-old kid with bleached hair, and Warren Day stared at it without a sign of recognition. I wouldn't have recognized it myself if I hadn't known whom I was looking for.

Kate Malone had almost told the truth with her last story. She had omitted only one item and changed one other. The part she left out was that she had served eight months of a two-year term in the girls' corrective home before being paroled. The part she changed was that her offense had not been shoplifting, but acting as lookout for a pair of bank

287

robbers — one of whom was her paramour.

I looked up at Day's puzzled face.

'I told this kid I wouldn't turn her in if she told me a straight story,' I said. 'But her story was a little bent. Better pick up Kate Malone.'

'The Lawson maid?' Day asked. 'Why?'

'Because she's the link we were talking about. The link with the underworld.' I tossed the picture to him. 'Take a closer look at Janet Whittier's picture.'

22

In spite of it being more than four hours after the time he was supposed to go off duty, there was no holding the inspector now that he scented a solution. Going into the outer office, he snapped a dozen orders at Desk Sergeant Danny Blake, all of which boiled down to two things — have Kate Malone brought in for questioning, and locate Lieutenant Hannegan, who was also off duty, and have him report in at once.

With the wheels in motion, there was nothing to do but wait.

'We may as well grab something to eat,' Day suggested. 'We got probably a half or three quarters of an hour now, and there's no telling when we'll get through questioning this girl.'

But I had dined with Day in restaurants before, and somehow I always ended up with the check. 'You go ahead,' I told him. 'I want to run over to El Patio and check on my client. I'll meet you back here in forty-five minutes.'

We parted in front of police headquarters, Day turning left in the direction of one of the cheapest restaurants in town, and me turning right toward a cab stand on the corner. I went on by the cab stand, however, continued into the next block, and entered a quiet, clean-looking restaurant. The restaurant had a public phone, and I used it to dial El Patio. I got hold of Fausta and satisfied myself that Grace was all right. I told her I probably would be held up all evening and to have Greene sleep across the doorway again.

'I'll be over in the morning,' I said.

'This makes three days' rent you owe me,' Fausta said. 'When will you come to take me out?'

'Most any night now,' I said noncommittally. 'See you in the morning.'

I found an empty booth, ordered dinner, and by the time I had finished a second cup of coffee, my forty-five minutes were nearly up.

As I started to climb the steps at police headquarters, Chief of Police George

Chester rushed out, followed by three uniformed cops.

George Chester was a tremendous man. His shoulders were great slabs of beef; he wore size eighteen collars and size fourteen shoes. Conservatively, I would have guessed his weight at three hundred. A few years ago, when he was a major in my outfit during the war, most of his weight had been muscle. But in his late forties it was rapidly turning to fat. Since the war George Chester's normal color had gradually become an unhealthy red, and in the July heat it approached purple. The last time I had seen him, I had noticed his slightly strained breathing and asked if his heart had been checked lately.

'Don't believe in doctors,' he had growled.

Now, as he lumbered down the steps, I held up one hand. 'Not in this heat, please, Chief. You'll burst a blood vessel.'

When he failed to slow down, I shifted sideways to avoid being run over, and it was then I noticed that of the three cops with him, two carried riot guns and the third carried a carbine.

'Can't stop, Manny!' Chief Chester yelled as he ran across the sidewalk like a charging rhinoceros. When he had squeezed his three hundred pounds into the back seat of a squad car labeled *Chief of Police*, he called back through the window, 'Look me up later.'

The other three cops threw themselves into the car, the motor roared, and it shot away from the curb with its siren beginning to wail.

I shrugged and started up the steps again just in time to be knocked down by another cop with a riot gun, who slammed through the door just as I reached it. I scrambled out of the way as about a half-dozen uniforms rushed by. None of their wearers bothered to stop and inquire if the fall had broken any bones.

As I climbed to my feet and brushed myself off, six or seven sirens began to scream. From the police garage entrance a hundred yards away, squad car after squad car rolled, each adding its wail to the others as it reached the street.

This time I approached the door

cautiously, stepped aside as I pulled it open, and peered inside before entering. No one was in sight except Desk Sergeant Danny Blake and Lieutenant Hannegan, who was leaning over Blake and shaking his finger under the sergeant's nose.

'What happened?' I asked. 'Somebody steal the jail?'

Neither paid any attention to me. 'You find him, and fast!' Hannegan yelled, at which Sergeant Blake, who was old enough to be Hannegan's father, yelled back, 'Yes, sir, Lieutenant! Where the hell am I supposed to look?'

Hannegan swung to me. 'Seen Day?' he snapped.

'Not in the last half hour. He's up the street eating.'

At that moment the front door jerked open and Warren Day shot in like a scared rabbit. 'Hannegan!' he yelled. 'Quit dawdling! Grab a walkie-talkie and let's go!' Hannegan disappeared down a corridor at a dead run.

'Inspector,' Danny Blake said diffidently, 'the Malone woman has skipped. I'm having all the stations checked.'

The inspector glared at him, turned the glare on me, and said, 'If you hadn't held out so long, Moon, we'd have this case cracked.' Then he snapped at Blake, 'How much of a start she got?'

'Over an hour. According to Mrs. Lawson, she called a taxi right after Moon left, packed while it was coming, and took off without even giving notice.'

'Fine,' Day said disgustedly. 'A lot of good checking the stations will do. Probably she had the taxi drop her at the ferry and is across the river into Illinois by now. It'll take an extradition order to get her back.' He eyed me glumly. 'I suppose you want to tag along on this.'

'Depends on where you're going.'

Realizing I didn't know what was going on, he said, 'Your two pals, Dude Garrity and Harry Sommerfield, are holed up on Front Street. They decided to fight.'

'I see,' I said, not really seeing at all. 'I thought it was at least an atom bomb attack.' I looked at his impatient face. 'But since when does the chief of police personally go gunning for hoodlums?'

'When they're cop killers,' he said

294

grimly. 'They got Dinny O'Keefe and Myron Goldstein when they tried to blast their way out.'

Now I understood perfectly. Cops don't like killers in the first place, but the cardinal crime in any cop's book is cop-killing. Once a hoodlum has that tag pinned on him, he might as well give up, for the search for him never dies until the killer dies, and the case is never transferred to the inactive file even though no trace of the cop killer is found for twenty years.

Hannegan returned with the strap of a walkie-talkie strung over his shoulder. The moment he came into sight, Day ran toward the door. I nudged in ahead of Hannegan and followed.

A prowl car containing a cop chauffeur idled its motor at the curb. When Day shot into the back seat, I shot in right next to him. Hannegan slipped his walkie-talkie to the floor at my feet and climbed in front next to the chauffeur.

'Front and Locust,' Day snapped. He turned to glare at me. 'There's only one reason I let you come along, Moon.'

'Yes?'

'Your gun-happy pals are barricaded on the top floor of a two-story tenement. They got a whole arsenal, including rifles and a Tommy gun.'

'So?'

'Somebody else is almost bound to get shot before we take them. Maybe it'll be you.'

As we roared across town, Chief Chester's voice on the car radio kept us informed of the situation. By number, prowl cars were being ordered in from all over the city and instructed to report to designated points. By following the directions, we were able to figure out he was placing his men in a huge square, four blocks along each edge, around the besieged hideout.

Two blocks from Front and Locust we ran into a police barricade. 'Sorry, sir,' a patrolman told Day. 'Chief's orders that no cars go beyond here.'

We got out, and Hannegan retrieved his walkie-talkie, this time pushing upward the aerial wand until it waved six feet over his head. We left the driver with the car and proceeded another block on foot.

Not a civilian was on the street, though we could see many faces peering at us from windows. There seemed to be no police on the street, either, but every doorway and alcove we passed contained at least one armed cop.

'Listen,' I said as we neared the corner a block away from Front and Locust, 'you sure you got the right address? We're the only people out in the open.'

'You heard the chief on the radio,' Day snapped. 'It's still more than a block away.'

The last building before the corner contained a deep doorway, and in the doorway was another cop. 'Step in here, sir,' he told Day. 'They can see you from there.'

At that moment a rifle bullet whanged against the cement sidewalk, ricocheted from the side of the building, and whirred off. It was still whirring when Day, Hannegan, and I smashed against our informant.

The doorway was an entrance to an upstairs apartment, and was deep enough to accommodate us all comfortably. When we had untangled ourselves, I took the position closest to the street.

'Where are they?' I asked.

The cop said, 'Second building from the corner on the other side of the street.'

Dropping full length, I peered out cautiously at ground level. By stretching the imagination, the second building could be construed as being at Front and Locust, for there were no other buildings between it and that intersection. Once there had been, as attested by three gaping foundations of buildings which had either been torn down or burned, but actually the gunmen's hideout was in the middle of the block. This side of it, between it and the corner building, stretched along a long vacant lot. The hideout itself seemed to be a four-family tenement and it was ideal for standing off a siege, for clear ground lay on all sides of it.

'They're on the roof now,' the policeman volunteered. 'We got some tear gas up there, but they have masks. That hideout was prepared for everything.'

Directly across the street another cop

crouched in an areaway listening to a walkie-talkie, and diagonally across two more policemen knelt on the sidewalk this side of the building. One of them was also equipped with a walkie-talkie.

I pulled my head back and asked, 'Anyone been in contact with them?'

'The chief talked to them over a loudspeaker,' the cop whose doorway we shared said. 'But all the answer he got was a submachine-gun volley. Guess they intend to go down shooting.'

'There goes the Lawson case, then,' I told Day. 'Unless you get someone in that building and take at least one of them alive.'

'Want to volunteer?' Day asked sourly.

'Not particularly.'

The inspector switched on Hannegan's instrument and said, 'Chief Chester, sir?'

I stood close to Day in time to hear a voice rasp back, 'Yes?'

'Inspector Day, sir. Any orders?'

'Not at the moment. You know the situation?'

'Yes, sir.'

'Any suggestions?'

Day hesitated a moment, glanced at me, then said, 'These men are key witnesses in the Lawson case. Any chance of taking them alive?'

'They don't want to be alive,' Chester said. 'They want to die like big shots, and they're going to get their wish. I'm not risking any more lives on them.'

'If we could get someone in the building . . . ' the inspector suggested tentatively.

'Want to volunteer?' the police chief barked.

'Not particularly, sir.'

George Chester's voice rasped, 'You wouldn't suggest your men do anything you wouldn't, would you?'

Day took the receiver from his ear, glared at it ferociously, replaced it again, and said in a choked voice, 'I'm ready any time you are, sir.' Then he stared at me over his glasses and added, 'The suggestion came from Manny Moon. He's here with me.'

'He is? Let me talk to Manny.' I took the handset and said, 'How are you, Chief?'

'Terrible. What you think, Manny?'

'I think you're missing a bet if you bump these guys off. The inspector didn't get a chance to finish, but we think we got the Lawson case figured out. But there's no evidence, and damn little chance of finding any. At the moment it looks like our only chance of a conviction is to make one of these gunnies talk. I think you ought to try to get someone into the building.'

'They're cop killers,' the chief grumbled. 'They don't deserve a chance.'

'You're running the show,' I told him. 'But three people have died in this Lawson affair, and another is hiding out to avoid becoming the fourth. Four people ought to get at least as much consideration as two cops.'

For a moment there was silence. 'All right, Manny,' he said suddenly. 'How do you suggest we get inside?'

I didn't like his emphasis on the word 'we.'

'I'm just a civilian,' I said cautiously. 'I'm not supposed to tell cops how to run their business.'

'You used to be in the infantry. Look at it as a tactical problem. The building's a strong point — '

'You used to be in the infantry, too,' I interrupted. 'And you were a major when I was a sergeant. Look at it as a tactical problem yourself.'

'I am,' he said. 'They're both on the roof, we think. Now if we could get inside, we could come up on them from underneath. I figure a heavy covering fire would pin them down until we — '

'Who is this 'we' you're talking about?' I broke in.

'You and me.'

'I'm not a cop!' I hollered.

'You suggested the operation,' he said. 'If you want these guys alive, you'll get in on it. I'm willing to take a chance along with you, but I'm certainly not going to order any of my men in there. Of course, I can't order you in, either. I'll try it alone. Let me talk to Day again.'

I could feel my ears redden. 'Damn you, Chester! Where are you?'

'Southeast corner of Front and Locust. Behind the corner house. Where are you?'

'A block from you, at the intersection north of them. Northwest corner.'

'Let me talk to Day.'

'Cut it out,' I said irritably. 'I'll go in with you. Let me work across the street to the house just north of theirs first, will you?'

'Check. Good boy. Like old times, isn't it?'

I grunted.

'Let us lay it down for half a minute, then make your run.'

I said, 'Check,' and handed the receiver to Hannegan.

Stretched flat, I again poked out my head and viewed the situation. The besieged building had seemed about seventy-five yards away the first time I looked, but now there seemed to be about seventy-five miles between me and it. The roof was flat and ringed by a high edge that formed a protective wall for the gunmen. As I watched I saw a long slim wand of metal which pointed straight up sway gently in the breeze.

Suddenly gunfire crashed from all directions at once, and the side of the building I was watching puffed tiny clouds of brick dust all along its face. I shouted to Day, 'They've got a receiving set of some kind up there! They've been listening in!'

I saw his lips form 'What?' but the roar of battle was too deafening to hear above.

'Never mind,' I yelled at him. I rose to a crouch, took a deep breath, and started to run.

For ten yards I ran straight at my goal, then started to zigzag. At the second zag something began to chip holes in the asphalt where my feet had been before I zigged. Above the roar of gunfire I couldn't hear the weapon firing, but I could see flashes from a ground-floor window, and too many holes were appearing in the street for it to be anything but a Tommy gun.

Fortunately Thompson submachine guns are not very accurate beyond fifty yards. I had started out at what I thought was full speed, but during the second half of the trip I'm sure I doubled my rate.

Diving between the two cops stationed behind the corner building, I collapsed with my back to the wall and waited for the barrage to stop. It stopped almost at once, leaving a silence so profound it almost hurt the ears.

One of the cops had a handset to his ear. 'Yes, sir,' he said. Then to me, 'They're starting again in one minute, and they'll hold their fire to the roof and second floor so as not to hit you and the chief. The chief says both of you will take off for the front door a half-minute after the barrage starts.'

'Tell him,' I said, 'they got a receiver up there and are listening in on his instructions. Also at least one of them isn't on the roof. He's on the ground floor with a Tommy gun.'

'Huh?' the cop said, and stared at me blankly.

'Tell him to hold the barrage,' I yelled at him.

'Huh? Listen — '

Jumping to my feet, I grabbed the handset from him. 'Chief — ' I got out, but the rest was drowned by an ear-shattering burst of fire.

I slammed the handset into the cop's stomach and he said, 'Oof!'

305

I felt like following it with my fist, for in thirty seconds big George Chester would be heading for the front entrance of the besieged building. And inside, waiting for him to come through the door, sat a killer with a submachine gun.

23

I hesitated between three possible courses of action. I could head for the hideout's front door as planned; I could reverse direction, cut around the back of the building now shielding me and hope to find some way of entering the rear of the hideout; or I could forget the whole thing and simply stand by while George Chester got himself killed.

The first alternative meant a fifty-yard dash through machine-gun fire. The second meant a slightly longer dash over broken, weed-grown ground which would make for much slower traveling than the smooth sidewalk in front. It also meant running directly under the nose of the rifleman on the roof, since I assumed he would be stationed at the rear of the building as long as his partner covered the front. The third alternative meant I might live longer, but I still had to live with myself.

The sweep-hand of my wrist watch told me the barrage had been underway fifteen seconds. Instead of waiting for the full thirty to pass, I turned and raced to the rear of the building. As I rounded the edge, I glanced back out of the corner of my eye just long enough to catch a glimpse of the cop with the walkie-talkie. He was shouting something impossible to hear over the roar of submachine guns, carbines, and riot guns, and pointing in the direction Chief Chester had told me to go.

I didn't bother to zigzag, hoping that since the besieged killers expected us both from the front thirty seconds after the barrage started, my early start and shift of direction might catch them off guard. The fifty yards from the rear of my building to the rear of the other seemed like fifty leagues. But even though handicapped by a false leg and with knee-high weeds clutching at my pants and holding me back as though I were wading through water, I'm sure I broke world records for the fifty-yard dash with that sprint.

The first-floor window sills were about shoulder-high from the ground, and the corner window facing me was raised from the bottom. As I neared it, I leaped into the air with both my legs and arms stretched out straight toward the side of the building.

The soles of my feet smacked the side of the building three feet off the ground, my knees bent, and my fingers clamped over the sill. I snapped my knees straight again, simultaneously pulled on the sill with all my strength, and literally hurtled into the room. I slid on my stomach across linoleum clear to the far wall.

I was in a kitchen, a fact I discovered by banging my head on a sink as I scrambled erect. At the same time I jerked Moldy Greene's .45 from under my arm and swung it at something cowering beneath the kitchen table.

The something proved to be a very scared middle-aged woman in a dirty house dress. There was no point in trying to say anything to her, for inside the building the noise was nearly as deafening as outside. And to it was added the crack of bullets smashing into the upper story and the screaming whine of ricochets.

Assuming that Dude Garrity and Harry the Horse had occupied only one of the four apartments before converting the whole building into a fortress, the thought flashed through my mind that perhaps a number of innocent persons might be caught in the other apartments. But I had enough to think about without worrying about their safety.

Cautiously I slipped out into the hallway. I sidled along the hall with the .45 thrust searchingly in front of me. The muzzle flashes I had seen placed the Tommy gun in the front room of the apartment I was in now. The hallway ran clear from the front room to a glass-paned door beyond the kitchen, and through the glass I could see this door led to a communal inside hallway, with stairs going both up to the second floor and down to the basement. Aside from the front room and kitchen, the apartment seemed to contain only two more rooms and a bath, all situated on the right side of the hallway.

I slipped past the open dining room

door after a quick glance within, past the bath and bedroom, then flattened myself against the wall outside the front room door, which was shut. I was not waiting for anything in particular — I think I must have been waiting for my mind to crack and leave me crazy enough to push open the door and face a spitting machine gun.

Abruptly there was an instantaneous pause in the firing, and before it resumed at full blast, I twisted the doorknob and slammed open the door.

My quarry was just starting to spin away from facing the front door as I swung my gun up. I'd intended to use my gun as a club, or else place a bullet in a non-vital spot in order to take my quarry alive; but when his weapon began to chatter, I forgot everything but self-defense.

The Tommy gun was cradled against his left hip, and apparently he had been firing it with one hand, for his right was in a sling.

It seemed to take me forever to center my pistol and press the trigger. Actually it must have been one of the fastest snap shots I ever got off, for Harry the Horse began to trigger his Tommy gun the same moment he began to spin. I fired after his burst started, and the burst continued for an instant or two after I fired. But the slugs he got off while I was squeezing the trigger hit the wall three feet to one side. The remainder climbed the wall and squirted across the ceiling as he toppled over on his back with a hole in his forehead.

I was so sure of that shot, I started racing for the rear stairs as soon as the gun kicked in my hand. At the second floor I reduced my speed to a cautious wriggling on my stomach, since lead was screaming through every window at this level. The stair-head brought me into another communal hall, except this one was shared by the two second-floor apartments. At its far end I could see another set of stairs for the use of the second upstairs apartment.

Directly in front of me was another glass-windowed door, but only slivers of glass remained in the shattered French panes. I wondered fleetingly if this had been the apartment rented by the two gunmen, and hoped that if it had not been, the tenants had been smart enough to run for the basement before the shooting started.

Halfway down the communal hall was a steep stairway leading to an open trap door in the roof. It was little more than a permanently fixed stepladder. Slowly I began to wriggle toward it, but just as I reached it, something smashed a hole in the third rung over my head, splashing splinters in my face. I spread flat again and tried to dig a dent in the floor with my chin.

All at once the firing began to diminish, then trickled off to a few scattered final shots. Jumping erect, I scurried up the ladder-like stairs. I shot through the trap door like a jack-in-the-box, landed heavily on graveled tar paper, and made two complete spins before I would believe I had the roof all to myself.

In the center of the roof stood the portable shortwave radio whose aerial I had seen from the street. It was on, but emitting only static. Brick chimneys thrust upward about five feet in from the edge of the roof on either side of the house. I circled these warily, but Dude Garrity was nowhere in evidence.

Just as I started back toward the trap door, I heard someone climbing the ladder and I faded behind one of the chimneys. My gun centered on the section of atmosphere where I judged the climber's head would appear, but I let the muzzle droop when a little blonde girl about ten years old stumbled out on the roof. She was in a sunsuit and bare feet, and tears of fright were streaming from her eyes. One side of her face was the flaming red that denoted a solid slap, and both her upper arms showed finger bruises. Pushing her from behind came Dude Garrity, a rifle at trail position in his right hand. His straw hat was missing, but he still wore his white suit and it was filthy with tar from the roof.

The girl blocked my aim until Garrity got clear of the stairs, and then he immediately grabbed her by the upper arm and jerked her spine against his stomach. At ten-foot range I undoubtedly could have placed a slug through Dude's shoulder without endangering his companion. But I would have hated to make a mistake and added a ten-year-old kid to the small list of corpses St. Peter is one day going to make me explain, and I couldn't take the chance. Instead I drew back and tried to make myself look like part of the chimney.

Garrity's rifle butt scraped the other side of the chimney as he went by. I shifted around to the side nearest the trap door and watched as he forced the little girl toward the roof edge overlooking the street. As he neared it, he went into a crouch, and six feet away he dropped to his knees, forcing the girl to hers also.

'The gravel is hot,' the kid said in a shaky voice, and began to sob.

'Shut up!' he snarled. His arm was across her back, and his fingers dug savagely into her shoulder, holding her rigidly against his side. 'Hey, cops!' he yelled.

After a few moments a loudspeaker boomed, 'Who's speaking?'

'Garrity!' shouted the gunman. 'You got my pal with a stray shot.'

Apparently he had found Harry and assumed the bullet in his head had come through the window. I was just beginning to crawl toward his back, with the intention of bringing my gun down on his head, when he spoke again.

'I got a young kid with me! You hear me, cops?'

'We hear you,' boomed the loudspeaker. 'Better give up, Garrity.'

The gunman laid down his rifle, rose to a crouch, and pushed the girl ahead of him to the roof edge. Her head just showed above it.

'Take a good look at this kid, cops!' Dude yelled. 'I'm walking out of here, and the kid with me. My gun will be in her side, and the first wrong move anyone makes — she gets it!'

Now I was halfway to the rifle lying behind Garrity on the graveled tar paper.

'Better give up, Garrity,' said the loudspeaker. 'You'll never make it out of this trap.'

At that moment the shortwave radio on

the roof sounded off. 'Stall him along,' came Warren Day's voice. 'Moon's in there somewhere.'

Dude Garrity whirled, and at the same moment I stopped creeping and started charging. Without releasing his grip on the girl, he shot his right hand under his arm.

I reached him just as his hammerless revolver appeared. Before he could swing the muzzle to bear on me, the barrel of my automatic cracked the back of his hand, and his gun skittered across the roof.

Dude swept his left arm forward, flinging the little girl head first into my stomach. We went down in a tangle, and by the time I pushed her out of my lap and rolled clear, Dude had the rifle and was swinging the muzzle toward me.

In my mind was the intention to shoot Garrity through the arm and make him drop his rifle, but as I rolled away from the child, his form was nothing to me but a large blur.

I pressed the trigger of my automatic before I stopped rolling, firing blindly at the blur. A fraction of a second later the rifle cracked, and a small hole appeared in the tar paper between me and the child.

Dude Garrity bent over slowly, then just as slowly began to straighten again. A red stain appeared in the center of his dirty white coat. His long, horsy face set in concentration as he forced the drooping rifle barrel up. Now I was seated, and could choose my target with more discrimination. I put a second slug through his right shoulder, and he spun completely around, dropped the rifle, and sat down with a thump.

He stared at me from eyes vacant with shock. His mouth drooped open, and red froth bubbled from one corner. Getting to my feet, I stood over him.

'Who hired you to bump Vance Logan, Dude?'

One hand supported him in his seated position, while the other lay limply in his lap. His voice was one wheeze ahead of a death rattle when he spoke. 'You're a bright boy, chum. Figure it out.'

Then he died sitting up.

I turned to the little girl, who had stood up and was lifting first one bare foot and then the other from the hot roof. She was sobbing steadily.

'Take it easy, honey,' I said. 'He can't hurt you now.' Then I raised my voice and yelled, 'Hey, cops!'

'Better give up!' boomed back the loudspeaker.

'It's Moon!' I yelled. 'Come on in and sort out the bodies.'

24

Instead of asking if I was all right, the first words the inspector spoke to me were, 'The idea was to take at least one of them alive! I ought to book you for destroying evidence.'

'I would have taken Garrity alive if you hadn't shot off your face into that walkie-talkie,' I snapped back at him.

The little girl turned out to be named Janet Mueller, and she was the daughter of the woman I had seen hiding under the kitchen table downstairs. The other tenants, two married couples and a total of seven children, we eventually found cowering in the coalbin.

The upper right-hand apartment proved to be the gunmen's hideout. I went through it with Warren Day, and I have never seen so much armament outside of a government arsenal. It took three cops just to carry out the ammunition. We also found gas masks and another shortwave radio.

It was at this point I remembered George Chester.

'He's at the hospital,' Day said. 'Had a slight heart attack just before the last barrage started.'

Hannegan stuck his head in the door, and the inspector asked, 'You phone the hospital?'

'Yes, sir,' Hannegan said. 'He's okay, but he's staying overnight.'

Then I started to get mad. 'The only reason I came in this hole was to keep the chief out of trouble,' I yelled. 'And all the time he was enjoying himself a heart attack!'

'Take it easy,' Day told me. 'There are some rewards on these guys, and I'll see that you get half.'

'And I will,' I informed him, 'see that I get the other half.'

We were getting ready to leave when the morgue wagon arrived. As attendants were hauling two long wicker baskets from its rear door, I walked into the lower front room for a final look at Harry Sommerfield.

He no longer looked tough. He seemed

smaller, somehow; curiously shrunken, as though even in death he was cowering from his hunters. The barrel of the Tommy gun lay across his left leg, and his bandaged right arm had slipped from its sling and thrust out from his body in a stiff right angle. I noted the tightly wound gauze ran from his shoulder to a point midway between his elbow and wrist, and seemed to cover a splint which held the arm at a rigid right angle, an observation which led me to the conclusion that my shot during our previous gun fight had broken the bone.

Then two men came into the room and casually dumped his body into a wicker basket.

It was nearly nine and the sun was beginning to set when we got back to headquarters. Warren Day collapsed behind his desk, looked at Hannegan as though surprised to see him still with us, and said, 'Go on home, Lieutenant.'

But as Hannegan turned to leave, Day changed his mind. 'Find out what developments there are on the Malone woman first.'

In a few minutes Hannegan was back with a report that Kate's taxi had been traced, and as the inspector had guessed, she had taken the ferry. Illinois police had been asked to pick her up, but so far had reported nothing.

'All right, Lieutenant,' Day said tiredly. 'Now you can go home.'

He sat looking at me glumly for a few moments after Hannegan departed. 'Looks like all we got left is the suicide note,' he said finally. 'Give the professor a ring.'

In the phone book I found Professor Quisby's number and dialed it. A woman answered.

'Professor Quisby, please,' I said.

'I'm sorry, but he's out for the evening. Is this Mr. Moon?'

I told her it was.

'I'm Professor Quisby's sister,' she said. 'He expected you to call earlier. He had a faculty meeting at eight-thirty. He asked you to leave a number and he'll phone in the morning.'

I gave her my apartment phone number, and hung up.

'I don't understand you,' Day said

suddenly. 'You know how to shoot. Why'd you have to knock both those guys off?'

'It happened too fast,' I said shortly.

'But you managed to put a bullet in Garrity's arm. Couldn't you leave it at that?'

'That was the second one,' I said. 'The first one did the damage.'

'You should have put the first one there,' he said insistently. 'Apparently you know how, because Sommerfield had a bullet in his arm, too, from your first encounter.'

'Next time there's a building full of killers, you can go in,' I said irritably. 'As a matter of fact, during our original clash I didn't aim at Harry's arm. I meant to puncture his head, not just give him a flesh wound.'

'It was more than a flesh wound by the looks of the bandage,' Day said.

I nodded. 'That kind of surprised me. I was almost sure at the time it was a minor wound, because he managed to drive the car away.' Then a thought struck me, and I sat up straight. 'Listen, I just had a wild idea.'

'What?'

'It's too wild to repeat. Let me use your phone some more.'

After using the phone book again, I dialed another number.

'City Hospital,' a male voice answered.

I told the man who I was and that I wanted to get in touch with Dr. Thomas Halloran.

'He's off duty till seven a.m.,' the voice said.

I got the phone number of intern quarters from him and eventually got Halloran to the phone.

'Manny Moon,' I told him. 'I sent you two shot-up hoodlums a little while ago. Seen them yet?'

'I heard about them. I'll see them in the morning.' He laughed in a deliberately ghoulish manner. 'Thanks for the business.'

It was supposed to be a joke, but I think he meant it. I said, 'Do me a favor and phone your report to my apartment as soon as you get it, will you?'

'Sure, Manny. Looking for anything in particular?

'Yes. The short one has a previous wound and is still bandaged up. I'd like to know if it was made by one bullet or two.'

His voice sounded puzzled. 'All right. Can do.' Then he brightened. 'I'll start about seven-thirty. Why don't you come down and watch?'

I told him I hated to miss the chance, but I always had breakfast at seven-thirty. Then I hung up.

'What was that double talk about two bullets?' Day wanted to know.

I grinned at him. 'That was for your benefit, Inspector. It isn't actually what I wanted to know at all.'

'Are you holding out again?' he demanded.

'Sure,' I admitted brazenly, before adding, 'But only overnight. I'll let you in on my wild idea after I hear from Halloran in the morning. Let's go home and go to bed.'

25

I keep my phone in my bedroom because many of the people I know stay up all night and think nothing of making phone calls at four in the morning. Although I get more phone calls during the day than at night, it requires much less energy to rise from an easy chair three or four times and walk into the bedroom than it does to climb out of bed even once, strap on my leg, and stagger half-asleep into the front room.

When the phone rang at eight a.m., I simply reached over and grabbed it without even bothering to wake up. 'Fumph,' I said intelligently.

'Tom Halloran,' a cheery voice said. 'You awake yet?'

'Partially now. Go ahead.'

'Both customers were D.O.A.,' he told me. 'The short one caught a bullet at the juncture of the frontal bones; it penetrated downward clear through the medulla oblongata and exited — '

'Wait a minute,' I interrupted. 'I know what killed the guy. All I'm interested in is his previous wound. Had his arm in a sling, didn't he?'

'That's right. Apparently a day-or-two-old gunshot wound. Shattered the right humerus. Seemed to be only one wound though.'

'That's all I expected,' I told him. 'That question about two bullets was just to confuse Warren Day. Would you say it was a serious wound?'

'He'd have gotten over it, if that's what you mean. Might have developed a stiff arm. A shattered bone is never exactly a minor injury.'

'Thanks,' I said. 'That's all I wanted to know.'

'The big guy's previous wound was a little more complicated,' he said.

'What previous wound?'

'He had a stomach wound about two weeks old. He still had a compress on it, and I'd say he hadn't been out of bed more than a week.'

'Thanks again,' I said. 'Call me any

time you need a fresh corpse.'

As soon as I hung up, I lifted the receiver again and phoned Homicide. 'Inspector Warren Day, please,' I said.

After a moment Day came to the phone. 'Yes?'

'Manny Moon,' I said.

'You're phoning from bed,' he accused. 'You couldn't possibly be up this early.'

'I've already done the laundry and got the kids off to school,' I told him. 'How's the chief this morning?'

'All right. I just phoned the hospital. He checks out in an hour. The doc wants him to rest at home today, but he'll be in tomorrow.'

'Glad to hear it,' I said. 'What you got that's recent on Dude Garrity and Harry Sommerfield?'

'About ten pages of teletype. One or the other was wanted everywhere but Greenland. Get specific.'

'Where would Garrity have picked up a stomach wound about two weeks ago?'

'Nowhere,' he said promptly. 'I got the record memorized.'

'Then recheck your memory,' I told

him. 'Doctor Tom Halloran just phoned me, and Garrity's got one. Do me a favor and recheck, eh?'

'All right,' he said grumpily. 'Drop down later on and maybe I'll have something. You hear from Quisby yet?'

'No. I'm going to phone him now.'

'Ring me back if he has anything,' Day said, and hung up in my ear.

The next call I made was to Fausta's apartment. Grace Lawson answered. 'Good morning,' I said. 'You people had breakfast yet?'

'Just getting ready to fix it.'

'Hold off a half hour and I'll join you,' I said.

'All right. I'll tell Fausta, but you better hurry. And listen, Mr. Moon — is it all right if Arnold comes up to see me here?'

'Not unless I'm there, too. Has he tried to?'

'He's downstairs now, but Mr. Greene won't let him up.'

'Good for Mr. Greene,' I said. 'See you in a half hour.'

I made another call, to Professor Laurence Quisby's house. His sister answered the phone.

'Laurence tried to phone you three times,' she said. 'But your line has been busy for fifteen minutes. He had to leave because he had an eight-thirty class, but he wants you to stop by the school.'

'Thanks,' I said. 'Do you happen to know if he deciphered the message?'

'Laurence never discusses his police business with me,' she said in a cool voice.

My last phone call before getting out of bed was for a taxi. In the fifteen minutes it took for it to arrive, I managed to shave, shower, and dress.

I got to El Patio about a quarter of nine. At the bottom of the stairs to Fausta's apartment I found two people. Moldy Greene sat on the third step with his arms folded. Glowering at him with his face red from anger was Arnold Tate.

I said, 'Good morning, gentlemen,' to which Moldy waved languidly and said, 'Hi, Sarge.'

Arnold swung around. 'Mr. Moon, will you tell this — this gentleman it's all right for me to see my wife?'

'Had breakfast?' I asked.

'I just had a cup of coffee. How can I eat when I don't know how Grace is? And why aren't you with her?'

'Mr. Greene and I are working shifts,' I told him. To Moldy I said, 'Let him go up. Breakfast ought to be ready by now, so he can't poison it.'

Grace greeted her husband as though they had been separated two years instead of two nights. They sat holding hands through the whole meal, hardly touching the pancakes and sausages Fausta went to the trouble of preparing. To make Fausta feel better, Moldy and I ate their shares.

'Why aren't you in school?' I asked Arnold when breakfast was disposed of.

'I cut,' he said. 'I can't study or sit in class or anything when I don't know whether or not Grace is in danger.'

Fausta went out to the hall in answer to a knock on the door and returned with the morning paper. She scanned the headlines, glanced up at me sharply, then continued to read, frowning deeper the further she read. 'Manny Moon!' she said when she had finished the item. 'Why did you try to get shot before you came to take me out?'

'I needed the reward money before I could afford you,' I said.

'Playing hero!' she said scornfully, and tossed the paper to Grace.

It went from hand to hand, with me getting it last. The write-up was page one and was bylined by the *Globe*'s top features-writer. It referred to my 'daring, singlehanded assault on two of the nation's most desper-ate criminals' and made me sound either like a movie-style hero or a suicidal idiot, I couldn't decide which.

Neither could the other persons present, apparently, for reactions were mixed. Grace turned starry-eyed with admiration, even shifting her attention temporarily from Arnold to me. Arnold examined me with a pecu-liar expression which indicated he thought I was mad, and Moldy Greene inquired, 'Those the same characters I almost got before you chased them away?'

'Yes,' I said. 'Want half the reward?'

'No, no,' he said magnanimously. 'After all, you was on the spot.'

At nine-thirty I left with Fausta and

Grace again in tow, after firmly telling Arnold to get back to school and stop worrying about his bride's safety. He reluctantly agreed only after Grace backed me up by appealing to the scholastic side of his nature.

'Suppose you failed a course, Arnold,' she said. 'You'd never get to be a university president, and I'd be so ashamed.'

My two female companions were dressed more conservatively today, Fausta wearing the same dirndl and peasant blouse she had discarded in favor of a sunsuit yesterday, and Grace wearing a backless sundress which exposed a good deal of her top, but at least covered her thighs. I still felt a bit like the manager of a burlesque house, but I lost the feeling that I should keep looking over my shoulder to see if the cops were raiding the joint.

At the State Teachers' College we caught Professor Quisby during a ten-minute break between classes. He handed me a typewritten paper without comment. It was a transcript of the complete note written by Don Lawson, and it read:

Dear Ann,

I hate to leave this way, because undoubtedly the publicity will be unpleasant for you, but I think it the wisest course. Explain things to Grace. Uncle Doug may be able to make you understand better, for he knows my condition. I can't stand to just sit and wait for death, so I'm going forward to meet it. I'm writing to you instead of [Here the word 'Kate' was scratched out] *Grace because you've been the only person aside from Uncle Doug and Maggie who ever made any attempt to understand me.*

Love, Don.

I read it over twice, then handed it to Grace and let her read it.

'Why it was suicide after all, then!' Grace said when she had finished. 'Why do you suppose someone cut off the bottom part?'

Professor Quisby cleared his throat. 'Perhaps,' he intoned, 'someone deliberately wanted it to look like murder.'

Fausta read the transcript, screwed up

her nose, and said, 'I think you made a lot of trouble for nothing. This is no more than you had before.'

'Let's see what Warren Day has to say about it,' I suggested.

We found the chief of Homicide in his office poring over teletypes for the last part of June and early July.

'I think I got it,' he greeted me when I opened his door in response to a shouted 'Come in!' His eyes bugged out as he saw Fausta's bare shoulders, then shifted to Grace's scanty sundress, and he blinked rapidly twice. 'Hello, hello,' he said in a faintly strangled voice. 'Come in and sit down.'

'What do you think you've got?' I inquired when we had all found chairs.

'Oh, yeah,' he said, coming back to earth. He inverted the teletype sheet and scanned it quickly. 'This is for June twenty-eighth,' he said. 'Two masked bandits tried to stick up the Central Trust Bank at Peoria, Illinois. A teller managed to sound the alarm, and they were beaten off without getting anything. One was believed to be wounded. They headed southwest, switched cars with a traveling salesman after knocking him out with a gun butt, and their trail was lost at the Illinois border. No one was able to give a very good description of the bandits, even as to size. You know how those things go; everybody sees something different. But at least two of the witnesses agreed that one was tall and the other short. And they all agreed that both were dressed either in white gabardine or Palm Beach.'

The inspector stopped and peered at me over his glasses.

'Could be our boys,' I said. 'And the date is only two and a half weeks back.' I tossed him the transcript of Don Lawson's suicide note.

When he had read it, he frowned at me and asked, 'What do you make of this?'

'What do you make of it?' I countered.

He read it again. 'Can't see a reason in the world why anyone would cut off the lower part. As far as the reference to Dr. Lawson is concerned, he himself told us young Don fancied he had every disease in the book, and called at his office regularly with fatal symptoms. We also knew Don didn't get on too well with his sister here, but was fond of Maggie and Ann — Mrs. Lawson. Think the maid could have cut it off because her name appeared and then was scratched through?'

'Not likely,' I said. 'She wouldn't have been able to tell what the scratched-out word was without a microscope.'

'Then I don't get it at all,' the inspector decided. 'Just offhand I'd say this pretty definitely establishes the boy's death as suicide, and knocks our last theory right in the head.' He glanced quickly at Grace, as though afraid she might know what the last theory was.

I shook my head. 'You can't get around Vance Logan's income and a certain other person's small bank account.'

Day frowned at me. 'You mean you still go for the theory you had yesterday?' Again he glanced at Grace self-consciously.

I nodded. 'I not only go for it. This clinches it. I'm sure who the murderer is.'

26

My remark drew a moment of dead silence from everyone. Grace was the first to speak. 'It isn't anyone we know, is it?' she asked inanely. Her face was suddenly white, and I felt a twinge of pity.

'I'm afraid it is,' I said gently.

Warren Day scratched his head uncertainly, glanced at Grace, and then averted his eyes. 'Since you've gone this far, you might as well tell her who it is.'

I cocked one eyebrow at him. 'We haven't a shred of evidence, and I can't afford to be sued for scandal-mongering. At least till I collect the reward money on Garrity and Sommerfield.'

'If you get any,' he said shortly. 'Most of the rewards were 'for information leading to arrest and conviction'. Besides destroying the only evidence we had, you cost yourself at least eight thousand bucks by being trigger-happy. So far we have only three bulletins offering rewards dead or alive, and they come to only twenty-one hundred dollars.'

I shrugged. 'So what's wrong with twenty-one hundred dollars?'

He lowered his glasses and gazed at me forbiddingly over them. 'It's customary in the department for at least half the reward money to go to the family of any cop killed during the operation. Two were killed in this one.' His lips pursed, and he said more slowly, 'Of course you're not in the department, and can be a heel if you want to.'

'Were both the cops who were killed married?'

'Sure. And with a total of five children.'

'All right,' I said irritably. 'Whatever there is, divide it between them.' To Fausta I said, 'For those dates we have, you just fell out of the formal-clothes league. You can wear what you have on.'

Her beautiful shoulders lifted and fell. 'I do not care. I am used to hamburgers and beer when you take me out, anyway.'

Day said, 'Listen, Moon, I want a word with you privately.' He turned to Grace and Fausta. 'Do you ladies mind stepping out in the main office a few minutes?'

When we were alone, the inspector said, 'Now we can talk without using code. Listen, I got an idea.'

'What?'

'If we pull Mrs. Lawson in without evidence, Jonathan Mannering will slap us with a writ of habeas corpus before we can even question her. Suppose we drop out to her home and throw what we got at her without making an arrest? Just possibly she might break wide open.'

'Suits me,' I said.

The inspector cleared his throat. 'Listen, Manny — ' His voice trailed off.

'What?' I asked cautiously. When Warren Day wants a favor, my name becomes 'Manny.' When he gives orders, it remains 'Moon.'

'I know this is a little irregular, but would you mind doing the talking to Mrs. Lawson?'

'Why? I have no official police position.'

'Well,' he said, flushing slightly, then ended lamely, 'I'll deputize you and make it official.'

'No, thanks.'

'Listen, Manny, it's not often I ask you a favor.'

I didn't say anything.

'It's not very much to ask. It's not that I'm afraid to tell her, understand. But you've got a knack for that sort of thing. I've often said to the chief, if there's one guy who knows how to worm a confession — '

'Cut it out,' I said briefly. 'I'll confront your ladylove.'

'She's not my ladylove!' Day shouted.

'All right. So she's just another suspect. But if I do it, I want to do it *my* way.'

'Sure, Manny,' he said, relieved. 'Any way you want.'

'Then I want everyone involved in this thing out to the Lawson estate this afternoon. That means Jonathan Mannering, Gerald Cushing, Abigail Stoltz, and Arnold Tate. I'll get Grace there, and the rest are already there.'

'You mean you're going to jump Mrs. Lawson in front of everybody?' he said in astonishment.

'I mean I want everyone there.'

342

'What you intending to pull?' he asked suspiciously.

'Nothing,' I said, rising. 'Go beard the lady yourself, if you don't like my way of doing it.'

'I like it fine,' he said hurriedly. 'Don't be so touchy. I'll have everybody lined up in the drawing room at three p.m. How's that?'

'Make it the veranda,' I suggested. 'It's cooler out there.'

Since it was nearly noon, my two female satellites and I took a cab to El Patio and had lunch there. Grace hardly ate a thing, being too concerned over the identity of whoever had been trying to kill her.

'Is it one of the servants?' she asked for the fifth time, then added quickly, 'I mean besides Maggie or Edmund or Jason?'

'That leaves Kate and Karl,' I said. 'Stop asking questions and eat. You didn't have any breakfast to speak of, either.'

Just before three we had Moldy Greene drive us over to the Lawson house in his convertible. I left him on guard over the several cars parked in the garage and on the courtyard, in the unlikely event that our killer might try an escape by automobile.

'Don't let anyone at all drive out of here without an okay from me first,' I instructed him.

'Check,' he said, eying the police car parked in front of his convertible dubiously.

'Except Inspector Warren Day,' I added quickly.

We found Inspector Day, accompanied by Hannegan, impatiently awaiting us on the front porch. All the people I had requested were gathered there, also. Ann and Douglas Lawson sat side by side on the canvas porch swing. Abigail Stoltz reclined in a canvas lawn chair. Gerald Cushing and Jonathan Mannering sat on straight canvas-backed chairs with wooden arm rests. Arnold Tate was seated on the railing, facing inward, but jumped to his feet when he saw Grace.

The four remaining servants stood, as did the inspector and Hannegan, though there were two more canvas chairs and a wicker settee still vacant. I glanced around at the group, noting nothing but polite curiosity on any of the faces except that of Gerald Cushing. Cushing seemed to be impatient, glancing at his watch twice in rapid succession.

'Well, get on with it,' Day said testily. To the group he explained, 'Moon here is temporarily in charge.' His eyes touched Ann, then shifted to the space between her and Dr. Lawson, and his tone disclaimed responsibility for anything which might now happen. 'I don't know what Moon intends to do, but for the moment he has the backing of the police department.'

Arnold Tate had led Grace over to the wicker settee, and they were seated together holding hands. I partially seated myself on the veranda rail, with my feet still flat on the floor, and Fausta perched on the rail by my side. I said, 'We've called this gathering for a specific purpose. Inspector Day and I finally know who is responsible for young Don's death and for the attempts on Grace.'

From the corner of my eye I could see the inspector flush, then his expression faded into a strained grimace of agreement.

'However, we haven't any proof,' I went on. 'If we made an arrest, I have no doubt the criminal could successfully beat the case in court, for there isn't a shred of evidence. The whole solution is based on logical deduction — largely by Inspector Day.'

No one said anything. Twelve faces were merely attentive. Hannegan's was inscrutable, and Day's indicated a struggle between a desire to take a bow and the wish that his name had been left out of things entirely.

'Also, if we made an arrest, undoubtedly we would be sued. After consulting on the matter, we felt the wisest course was to gather together this group and explain what the criminal's motive and method of operation has been. Once all of you understand everything, the whole carefully built plot falls apart, for this has been a peculiar series of crimes, and the most peculiar thing about them is that the criminal will be unable to reap any benefit from them the minute you all understand what the crimes actually are.

'That is the sole purpose for which we called this meeting. If we brought the guilty person to trial, there is little doubt in my mind any jury would render a verdict of acquittal on the grounds of insufficient evidence. I'm also sure in my mind that even though acquitted by a jury, the killer would be convicted in the minds of all of you here. Therefore by airing the whole matter among this select group, we accomplish the same thing as we would by an arrest, but escape the probability of being sued.'

Inspector Day blurted, 'Will you get on with it, Moon!'

I continued unhurriedly, 'In the first place, practically nothing in this case was what it at first seemed. The attempts on Grace Lawson, for instance, were not attempts at murder at all. She was never in the slightest danger.'

'What?' Arnold Tate half-shouted. Twelve faces swiveled at Arnold, then turned back to me. Hannegan remained expressionless, and Day's suddenly furious eyes were fixed unwaveringly on my face.

I continued slowly, 'Going backward, Don's death was neither suicide nor murder, but a combination of both. Legally I suppose it was suicide, but morally it was murder. And going all the way back to the beginning, Donald Lawson Senior's death was not an accident, but deliberate murder.'

Ann Lawson emitted a gasp which drew everyone's eyes to her.

'You must understand everything I intend to tell you is based on hypothesis. It wouldn't stand up in court for a minute. But we know certain facts, and by combining them in proper order, we can arrive at a series of logical conclusions I'm sure you'll all agree with.

'First for the facts. Donald Lawson Senior was killed last August in an auto accident during which both the chauffeur Vance Logan and Doctor Douglas Lawson were injured. Six months ago Vance Logan began receiving an income in excess of ten thousand dollars a month, though he had no apparent means of support. The logical conclusion is that Logan was blackmailing someone. An off-the-record check of the resources of all those present showed some interesting things.' I paused and looked at Ann Lawson. 'For instance, how does it happen your total resources are only three thousand dollars, when you have income from a half million?'

Jonathan Mannering sat up straight, sputtering, 'Young man — in the first place you had no business prying into Mrs. Lawson's affairs. In the second place, if you employed the logic you seem to be so proud of, you would realize the will was probated only about six months ago. Mrs. Lawson's trust fund has been safely invested at an average of three-and-a-half-percent interest, but there hasn't been a dividend payment yet.'

'And also, Mrs. Lawson,' I said, ignoring the interruption, 'some time back you invested a hundred thousand dollars in Marsh Chemicals and sold out for a hundred and ten thousand. Mind telling what happened to that money?'

'Mr. Moon,' Jonathan Mannering said ominously, 'as Mrs. Lawson's attorney, I want to warn you any further inferences that my client has been paying blackmail will get you a suit for defamation of character.' He glanced around at the group, then added, 'However, I feel this should be clarified right now, before wagging tongues do any damage. That Marsh Chemicals transaction took place more than a year ago, just before Donald Lawson's death. Donald didn't want to appear in the matter, so he bought the stock in his wife's name, a quite common business procedure. Ann never even saw the money.'

Day's mouth had fallen open. He snapped it shut and glared at me with dawning suspicion.

'Thank you,' I said gravely. 'That clears that up. Getting on to the next fact, two professional killers named Dude Garrity and Harry Sommerfield murdered Vance Logan. Yesterday both were killed in a gun battle, as you may have read in the paper. They also had attempted to murder me, presumably because I was endangering the main criminal's security. However, they showed a marked antipathy to harming Grace Lawson, which indicated they had definite instructions to let her alone.'

Suddenly I turned my attention to Gerald Cushing. 'If you wanted to hire two professional killers, Mr. Cushing, how would you go about it?'

At first he looked startled, then faintly indignant. 'I'm afraid I don't follow.'

'I'm not trying to involve you in anything,' I said. 'Just take it as a hypothetical question. Where would you contact professional killers?'

'I haven't the slightest idea.'

'*Exactly*,' I said. 'Would you, Mrs. Lawson?'

Ann shook her head.

'Or you, Mr. Mannering?'

'Of course not,' the lawyer said, outraged.

I said, 'I won't bother to complete the circuit. The point I'm trying to make is that the average person couldn't get in contact with two killers such as Dude Garrity and Harry Sommerfield even if he had the desire. For a time we thought Kate Malone was the underworld contact, and was somehow tied in with this, but apparently her reason for skipping was fear of serving out a sentence for parole violation. We suddenly realized who the killer was when we discovered Dude Garrity had a two-week-old gunshot wound. And that is what puts the finger on our killer. Only one person here could possibly have come in contact with the pair.'

Now I still had twelve expressions puzzled, but Day's had changed. A light was beginning to replace the suspicion in his eyes.

'June twenty-eighth,' I said, 'Dude Garrity and Harry Sommerfield unsuccessfully tried to rob a bank in Peoria, Illinois. Garrity was wounded. The bandits headed in this direction and were lost track of not twenty miles from here. Somewhere Garrity managed to get his wound dressed, and when his companion was subsequently wounded last Sunday, he also managed to get medical attention without the treatment being reported to the police.'

After a moment of strained silence, all eyes focused on Dr. Douglas Lawson.

Ann rose and said in a choked voice, 'What are you getting at?'

'Just what you think,' I said. 'Garrity needed medical attention. He probably got it while his companion held a gun on the doctor. And sometime while the doctor was patching the patient up, he suddenly realized the two gunmen were an answer to his problem. All reputable doctors report to police the treatment of gunshot wounds. Instead of making a report, Dr. Douglas Lawson made a deal with his patient and his companion.'

27

Dr. Lawson said calmly, 'That's a pretty strong statement, Moon. You may get yourself a defamation of character suit yet.'

I shook my head at him. 'That would force us to bring you to trial. My bet is that you won't make a move that might spread the story of your guilt beyond this group here.'

Ann moved away two steps, clasped her hands in front of her and stared down at her brother-in-law. 'You didn't, Douglas! Say you didn't!'

'But he did,' I put in before the doctor could speak. 'Here's another fact for you. Your husband's death certificate shows a broken neck — no other injuries! Anyone whose head hit a windshield hard enough to break his neck would almost certainly have at least a brain concussion.' I turned my eyes on Douglas Lawson. 'On the spur of the moment you took advantage of a perfect situation and killed your brother, didn't you? I suppose you thought the chauffeur was unconscious, until he approached you a few months later and started nicking you for everything you had. Was that about how it happened?'

'How much can I sue this nitwit for, Jonathan?' Dr. Lawson drawled.

But Jonathan Mannering had his attention concentrated on me, and seemed unwilling to divert it.

'Your big brother was your father and childhood hero rolled into one, was he?' I shot at the doctor. 'Or was he the overpowering guy who refused to let you work as he had, who sent you to medical school because *he* wanted you to go, who planned your life and thought he was being kind to his kid brother, but was only building within you a hate that ended in murder?'

I paused for breath. 'After you started in practice you never saw much of your brother until he married the second time, did you? But when Ann became the hostess, you were a regular weekend guest. Your brother not only ran your life from infancy, he married the only woman you ever wanted, didn't he? And when the opportunity was suddenly thrown in your lap, you murdered him.'

Dr. Lawson's lips were still mocking, but his face was dead white. Every eye was turned on him. With an effort he lifted his own eyes to Ann, then swung them back to me. 'Go on with the rest of it,' he said softly.

'Probably you only wanted Ann at first. No doubt you knew the terms of the will, being so close to your brother, and figured the money was beyond your reach, anyway. Then Don started coming to you for treatment of imaginary ailments, and you recognized he had a neurotic personality. When the inspector and I interviewed you after the discovery of Don's body, you made the statement that you were not a psychiatrist. Technically I suppose you're not, but you had a year's graduate work in psychiatry at your brother's expense.

'About the same time Don started coming to you, Grace approached you with her marriage plans, and you suddenly saw a way to get both Ann and the money. Deliberately you encouraged the marriage, and you told Don he had an incurable disease — probably leukemia, since Don mentioned that disease to Arnold Tate.

'There's no way of finding out how you worked on Don's sensitive mind, but you managed to destroy it, and he plunged to his death. No court could convict you of murdering your nephew, but morally it was just as much murder as when you snapped your brother's neck. You changed the suicide note because it pointed to what you had done. Would you like to hear what Don actually wrote before you cut half the note off with a pair of scissors?'

I produced Professor Quisby's transcript and read it slowly. When I finished, the doctor's sardonic smile had faded and sweat stood out upon his upper lip.

'You didn't have to kill Grace,' I hammered at him. 'All you had to do was expose her secret marriage. But if you exposed it yourself, Grace would never forgive you, and you were too fond of her to risk that. You mentioned it to Ann and found you were on delicate ground there, too, for if Ann suspected you were being unfair to Grace, she would have dropped you like a hot potato. This would have ruined your whole chess game, for your final move in getting your hands on the Lawson estate was to have been your marriage to Ann. And you couldn't run the risk of exciting Ann's suspicion that you were trying to make her an heiress.

'So you went to work on Arnold Tate. Mysterious attempts were made on Grace's life, but strangely enough you were always around to block them. The first time, when the saddle girth broke, you even pointedly suggested someone had tried to kill her, a thought that hadn't occurred to Arnold or Grace until you mentioned it. The falling flowerpot conveniently missed her by several feet, and as I remember, it was you who first noticed the strong odor of her milk, making sure she didn't taste it.

'Then came the cut steering mechanism. Knowing Grace's jolting method of leaving the garage, you assumed it would break immediately and no one would be hurt, but just to make sure you came along for the ride, so you could control the situation.

'But the swimming pool incident was the masterpiece. Had she actually been thrown into the pool unconscious, Grace would have been bound to absorb *some* water, particularly if she were floating halfway to the bottom when you arrived, as you claimed. What really happened is that you simply dipped her in long enough to get her wet, pulled her out again, then yelled and dived into the pool.

'The clincher,' I went on, 'is your bank account. You have twenty thousand dollars to your name. Yet you've had a large income from your practice for eleven years, and six months ago inherited fifty thousand dollars. I imagine your original deal with Garrity and Sommerfield was only to murder Vance Logan and stop the draining of your resources, but once you had them lined up, you decided to use them for miscellaneous purposes, like ridding yourself of troublesome bodyguards.'

Running out of words, I took a deep breath and asked, 'Any important points I've left out?'

Dr. Lawson rose to his feet. His face was pale and his hands trembled, but his voice was still steady when he spoke. 'I think you've covered everything admirably, Mr. Moon. The only criticism I have to make is that it's all hypothesis, just as you yourself admitted before you began.' His voice rose slightly. 'And it's all hogwash! You haven't the faintest bit of evidence.'

'Never said I had,' I told him. 'If I had evidence, you'd be in jail now.'

The doctor mustered a deprecating smile and turned to Grace. 'You haven't swallowed any of this rot, have you, honey?'

Grace cowered back against her husband's shoulder. She made no reply, but the expression of horror with which she regarded her uncle was enough answer for him. His smile flickered out, and his face suddenly became pinched. With the movements of a sleepwalker, he faced his fiancée.

'Ann,' he said simply.

She backed away from him, put both palms to her face, and burst into tears.

Jonathan Mannering and Gerald Cushing simultaneously rose and approached her, making comforting noises from either side. Impatiently she shook them off, stared for a moment at Douglas Lawson as though at a stranger, then walked determinedly toward me.

'I hate you,' she said distinctly.

With that she burst into tears anew, rushed at Warren Day, and collapsed against his chest.

The inspector stood stiffly at attention, his arms held out from his body, at an angle as though to maintain balance. Above Ann's bowed head his face was the color of stewed beets, and the look in his eye that of a cornered rabbit. One hand made an indefinite motion toward the weeping woman's shoulder, then fell limply to his side before he could bring himself to administer a soothing pat. He remained in the same position, gaping like a fish, even after Ann suddenly left his inhospitable chest and disappeared into the house.

Douglas Lawson looked appealingly at Abigail Stoltz. She rose from her reclining position and followed Ann into the house without even glancing at the doctor. Without much hope he turned his eyes first to his friend Jonathan Mannering and then to Gerald Cushing, meeting nothing but a sort of horrified contempt in the face of either.

The doctor straightened his shoulders, managed the shadow of his former sardonic smile, and moved toward the porch steps. Maggie and Jason both moved out of his way. Then the inspector awoke from the coma he had been thrown into by Ann. 'Hey!' he said. 'Where you think you're going?'

'Home,' Dr. Lawson said. 'I don't seem to be very popular around here.'

'Guess again, friend,' Day said grimly. 'You're going down to headquarters.' The inspector glared over at me. 'Why Moon handed out the impression we weren't going to arrest you, I don't know, but Moon doesn't happen to run Homicide.'

I asked, 'What charge you bringing, Inspector?'

'Murder!' he snapped, regarding me as though he thought I were half-witted.

'Whose?' I asked.

'His brother, for one.'

I shook my head patiently. 'Not unless you get a confession. The only witness is dead.'

'Then we'll get him for his nephew's death. We've got the suicide note for evidence.'

'Which proves it was suicide,' I told him. 'You'll have a sweet time convincing a jury Dr. Lawson was responsible, unless he admits it.'

'Then we'll book him for attempted murder!' he yelled.

'Of Grace?' I asked. 'Sorry, Inspector. There was no intent to kill. The most you could convict him of is practical joking.'

'If you gentlemen have finished your discussion, I'll go along now,' Dr. Lawson said. Calmly he moved down the steps and walked toward the drive at the side of the house while the inspector watched speechlessly.

'You knew this all along, Moon!' he barked at me suddenly. 'You told a lie. You said you still believed the theory you had yesterday.'

'This *is* the theory I had yesterday,' I said calmly. 'You never asked me what theory I meant. But take it easy, Inspector. Dr. Lawson isn't going anywhere. Moldy Greene is back there in the courtyard where the doctor's car is, and has instructions not to let anyone but you drive out of the place. Let him think it over awhile, then run him in and go to work on him. He may break, and that's the only chance you got.'

'Fat chance,' he said, taking a large handkerchief from his pocket and mopping his brow.

Moldy Greene came ambling around the side of the house. 'Hey, Sarge — ' he started to say, when I broke in.

'I thought I told you to stay back there and prevent anyone from driving out. The killer's back there now!'

'Was he the guy you been looking for?' Moldy asked. 'That's too bad, because he ain't going to be much good to you now. He just jumped off the bluff.'

'What?' I yelled.

'Well, gee, Sarge,' Greene said defensively. 'All you said was to keep guys from driving out. You didn't say nothing about stopping them from doing anything else.'

At the end of August I got a card inviting me to Arnold Tate's graduation exercises. I sent a small present, but I didn't bother to go.

It was another two months before I heard anything more about any of the Lawsons, and then I got a phone call from Warren Day. 'Hey,' he greeted me in a strained voice. 'You still go around with that Fausta Moreni?'

'Some,' I admitted. 'Why?'

The inspector's voice sounded embarrassed. 'I wondered if maybe you and she might not be busy tomorrow night.'

'I can ask her,' I said. 'Is this an invitation?'

'Well, in a way. I thought maybe we might have dinner together somewhere.' Then he added hurriedly, 'I don't mean I'm inviting you out. You pay your check and I'll pay mine. Sort of a double date.'

'Why, Inspector,' I said in amazement, 'you mean you're actually taking a woman to dinner? And paying her part of the check? Anyone I know?'

'Well, yes.' He sounded embarrassed again. 'Ann — I mean, Mrs. Lawson.'

I was still sitting there stunned, when he spoke again.

'Listen,' he said. 'That girl of yours owns El Patio, doesn't she? If we had dinner there, do you think we could get a special rate?'